Why had she ever thought she could trust him?

Lauren's eyes traveled up Bill's shirt to his chin, over the faint scar on his tanned cheek and to his hooded eyes, which were focused on some point over her head. As she watched, the corners of his lips turned up just a fraction. When his gaze connected with hers, his ironic smile deepened.

"If you ever decide you can trust me again, give me a call," he said in a low voice. He grabbed her hand and the pad of his thumb stroked a line of heat across her wrist.

"I will," Lauren whispered as he dropped her hand.

But she knew she'd be a fool to trust him—or to call him again. So, why—as he turned and left her office—did she feel as if her heart was about to break?

D0720201

Dear Reader,

Be prepared to meet a "Woman of Mystery"!

This month, we're proud to bring you another new author, in our ongoing WOMEN OF MYSTERY program, which is designed to bring you the debut books of writers new to Harlequin Intrigue.

Meet Madeline St. Claire, author of *Private Eyes*.

Driven by the desire to create, Madeline St. Claire explored careers in interior design and fashion before discovering her real love: writing novels of romance and suspense. She still practices the art of "decorating on a budget" in the home she and her husband have nicknamed Bear Cottage.

We're dedicated to bringing you the best new authors, the freshest new voices. Be on the lookout for more "WOMEN OF MYSTERY"!

Sincerely,

Debra Matteucci
Senior Editor and Editorial Coordinator
Harlequin Books
300 E. 42nd Street, Sixth Floor
New York, NY 10017

Private Eyes
Madeline St. Claire

Harlequin Books

TORONTO • NEW YORK • LONDON
AMSTERDAM • PARIS • SYDNEY • HAMBURG
STOCKHOLM • ATHENS • TOKYO • MILAN
MADRID • WARSAW • BUDAPEST • AUCKLAND

If you purchased this book without a cover you should be aware that this book is stolen property. It was reported as "unsold and destroyed" to the publisher, and neither the author nor the publisher has received any payment for this "stripped book."

For Rob, the love of my life

ISBN 0-373-22299-8

PRIVATE EYES

Copyright © 1994 by Madeline St. Claire

All rights reserved. Except for use in any review, the reproduction or utilization of this work in whole or in part in any form by any electronic, mechanical or other means, now known or hereafter invented, including xerography, photocopying and recording, or in any information storage or retrieval system, is forbidden without the written permission of the publisher, Harlequin Enterprises Limited, 225 Duncan Mill Road, Don Mills, Ontario, Canada M3B 3K9.

All characters in this book have no existence outside the imagination of the author and have no relation whatsoever to anyone bearing the same name or names. They are not even distantly inspired by any individual known or unknown to the author, and all incidents are pure invention.

This edition published by arrangement with Harlequin Enterprises B.V.

® and TM are trademarks of the publisher. Trademarks indicated with ® are registered in the United States Patent and Trademark Office, the Canadian Trade Marks Office and in other countries.

Printed in U.S.A.

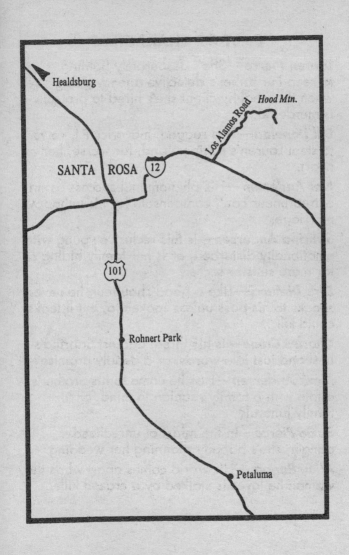

CAST OF CHARACTERS

Lauren Pierce—She's desperately fighting to keep her father's detective agency going when the wealthy client she's hired to protect is murdered.

Bill Donelan—This rugged, maverick P.I. vows to steal Lauren's business and, far worse, her heart.

Nat Andersen—His phenomenal success as an entrepreneur can't compensate for his unhappy marriage.

Sabrina Andersen—Is this reclusive young wife emotionally disturbed, or is her family hiding a far more sinister secret?

Dirk DiMucci—Like a good chauffeur, he never speaks to his boss unless spoken to, but if looks could kill...

Charles Caine—Is his threat against Sabrina's husband just idle words, or a deadly promise?

Mark Andersen—Has he come to his brother's estate with a family reunion in mind, or a family funeral?

Suzie Pierce—In the midst of unrealized danger, she's happily planning her wedding.

Allen Rogers—His world comes apart when the woman he loves is stalked by a crazed killer.

Chapter One

"I need you to pose as my girlfriend," said Nathaniel Andersen.

"Excuse me?" Lauren Pierce's brow puckered as she studied the handsome, Nordic-looking man seated across from her desk. The first thing that struck her when he entered her Santa Rosa private investigation office was his height—he was well over six feet, with a trim build. From his loafers and navy corduroy sports coat, which were casual but expensive, and from his air, which was relaxed and undeniably confident, she could tell he was probably wealthy. He might be just the well-heeled client she was looking for. However, his request for services was a bit out of her line.

"I know what I'm asking must sound strange," he said, "but I need a woman to pose as my girlfriend. You see, I need a divorce from my wife, and the best way to go about it, in this instance, is to convince her I'm involved with someone else."

The office door was closed, but the sounds of traffic drifted up through the window behind Lauren from

the busy street a story below. After working in this
office for her father for so many years, she was no
longer conscious of the noise. "Did you know that
you don't need to prove infidelity in California to get
a divorce?" she asked Andersen. "Irreconcilable differences arc enough. If you want a divorce, your wife
can't even contest it. If you say the two of you are
hopelessly incompatible and she says you're not, the
judge will take that dispute in itself as proof of irreconcilable differences."

"I know, but I don't want to be the one to ask for a
divorce. You see, divorce is looked down upon
strongly in her family. If I simply said, 'We're not
happy together, I'm divorcing you,' Sabrina's parents
would think it was her fault and the blame would come
down on her. Sabrina already has problems with her
mother, and I don't want to make them worse."

Lauren raised the ballpoint pen she was holding to
her lips. "But wouldn't it be just as humiliating for her
to discover you're seeing another woman?"

"No, because in that case I'm the cad, you see. She
can tell her family she's done everything possible to
make me happy, but I'm just a gigolo who can't stay
away from other women. They'll understand that and
sympathize with Sabrina, and it will make the divorce
easier for her."

Lauren leaned back in the vinyl executive chair.
Nathaniel Andersen was strikingly fair: blond hair and
eyebrows that lightened to corn silk above ice-blue
eyes made warm by his easy smile. If he was unhappily married, an attractive man like this, with a

smooth, open manner, probably already had women on the side. And his name was familiar. Where had she heard it before, just recently?

"I guess I see your logic," she said, not wanting to dismiss him as a potential client immediately. There was more she needed to know. "It sounds like you care a great deal about your wife's feelings, Mr. Andersen. But if you're that concerned for her welfare, why do you want a divorce?"

Lauren's voice conveyed only professional detachment. Still, for the first time, Andersen appeared uncomfortable. "My wife isn't...she's not a healthy woman." He shifted slightly in his seat. "Before we married, I suspected there might be something wrong with Sabrina, but I pushed the thought away, hoping she'd be different once she was away from the domination of her parents. But she has a problem with chronic, clinical depression, and she's under the constant care of a psychiatrist." He glanced down at his cuff and muttered, "She practically lives in the doctor's office." He looked up again. "I've come to the conclusion that, in a perverse way, she enjoys being sick. I've done all I can personally to try to bring her out of it, and she's been to specialists—I'm in a position to afford the best—but after eight years of battling this, I realize things aren't going to change.

"I'll be frank with you, Ms. Pierce, knowing that what I tell you is in strictest confidence...."

Lauren nodded as she watched him with grave eyes.

"We've had separate bedrooms for most of our married life. I'm an active man, I'm only thirty-two, and I can't stand the thought of living the rest of my life virtually alone. I want a woman I can share my life with, my work, someone I can relate to and give to emotionally. I need a companion, and Sabrina will never be that to me." He paused for a moment and ran his hand through his short, fine hair. "Sabrina is so self-absorbed I can't think she's any better off with me than apart from me. She's wealthy in her own right— her father is Joseph Falletti, who owns the Falletti Winery in Sonoma—so she won't lose anything financially by divorcing me."

Lauren was still skeptical. "There's a legitimate female escort service here in Santa Rosa. If you don't want to ask a friend to act for you, why not hire someone from a service? Besides, I'm sure their fees would be lower than what you'd pay me as a private investigator."

"I was just coming to that. Sabrina's family is old-world Italian and filled with temperamental types. When they discover I'm seeing another woman, there may be some initial anger, some flying off the handle. I don't really expect overt violence, but it's not a possibility I can rule out one hundred percent. I've done some checking on you. I know you're a brown belt in karate, so you can take care of yourself. I'd feel better hiring you than a model who's just trying to make some money on the side, or worse, a prostitute." He frowned in distaste.

Lauren's elbows rested on the arms of her chair and she tapped her pursed lips with steepled fingertips. She didn't like the idea of playing girlfriend to a married

man, but her age and good looks would make it easy
to pull off the role convincingly. Several times, mod-
eling scouts had approached her in public places and
pressed their cards on her, but she'd never felt the
slightest enthusiasm for that kind of work. What she
was interested in was keeping her father's detective
agency afloat.

"How long would you need my services?" she
asked.

"Only until Sabrina finds out about 'us.' It
shouldn't take long. You'd have to accompany me out
to dinner, dancing, away on weekends. Though my
scheme sounds unorthodox, I'm a moral man," he
hastened to assure her. "I've never stepped out on
Sabrina, and I'm not going to start dating until after
the divorce comes through, so you needn't worry I'll
try to take unprofessional advantage of our business
relationship."

"I'm glad to hear it," Lauren said firmly, but followed it with a smile to keep his goodwill. The phone
on her desk rang twice, and she realized her secretary
must have gone to lunch. With a murmured apology
she picked up the receiver.

It was only a telemarketer hawking subscriptions to
the local newspaper, but Lauren wanted a moment
alone to think. "I'm sorry, but this is an emergency,"
she told Andersen, putting the caller on hold. "Would
you mind waiting out in the reception area for a moment?"

"No, not at all." He rose and went out, closing the
door behind him.

She told the salesman she already received the *Press Democrat* at home and hung up, then swung her chair toward the venetian blind and focused on Andersen's proposal. She didn't usually take domestic cases, not because they were particularly dangerous, but because clients got angry when they paid you to dig up dirt on their spouses and there wasn't any to find. But this wasn't your usual divorce case, even if the players were the same.

The whole setup was so strange it made her feel edgy, but there was no denying she could use the money. Her father's firm had suffered, along with everyone else, during the recession. But unlike other businesses that had survived and were beginning to bounce back, the P.I. industry was slower to recover. Pierce Investigations had been just holding its own when her father passed away a year ago.

With her father gone and Lauren at the helm, she'd initially lost some clients who thought she was either too female or too young to be a competent P.I. As business dwindled, she'd had to let the agency's other full-time investigator go. She seldom had enough work these days to call in either of the two free-lancers who helped her on an as-needed basis.

This wasn't the time to turn clients away, but Lauren felt vaguely guilty at the thought of breaking up another woman's marriage. Still, she reasoned with herself, plenty of people today who wanted divorces were better off for splitting up, so who was she to say Nathaniel Andersen wouldn't be? It was an ambiguous question, but one thing was for certain, what she would make on this job would pay February's rent and then some.

Christmas dinner was just ten days behind her, and it had been a grim affair she'd have been happy to forget—if she could. Her mother, who'd never been very affectionate with her to begin with, had been in a critical, argumentative mood. Lauren had set her face in what she hoped was a calm, neutral expression and tried to concentrate on the Christmas carols playing on the stereo as her younger sister, Suzie, passed the serving dishes. But despite Lauren's devout prayers, their mother soon steered the conversation to one of her favorite topics—Lauren's lack of skill in managing her father's detective agency.

As Lauren struggled to swallow the moist turkey and creamy mashed potatoes, her mother stated flatly what she'd been implying for months—that Lauren was running Pierce Investigations into the ground.

Lauren hadn't argued; she knew it would only upset her mother further and make things worse. Instead, she tried to tell herself Mother didn't mean to hurt her. She was still overwrought by Dad's death, and Christmas was a hard time for everyone.

But despite all Lauren's attempts at rationalization, she'd felt the pressure of tears begin to build behind her eyes. *I will not cry,* Lauren had told herself, keeping her back rigidly straight.

"Why don't you just admit defeat, Lauren?" her mother had harangued, oblivious to her distress. "Go out and get a decent job working in an office or a bank or something. You'll never make it as a private detective!"

Recalling her mother's complete lack of faith in her, Lauren felt the pain afresh. She pushed her chair back to face her desk, trying to dispel the feeling. Then, suddenly, a picture came to her, and she even managed a ghost of a smile. If her father had been there at Christmas dinner, and she felt in an odd way that he had, she knew what he would have said to his wife. "Bull puckey!"

Lauren rose resolutely and walked to her office door. Andersen looked up from the chair where he'd been patiently reading a copy of *Time*. "Won't you step back in, Mr. Andersen?"

HE AGREED to her fifty-dollar hourly fee without a qualm and gave her ten crisp one-hundred-dollar bills as a deposit. When she asked for photos of the Falletti family, he pulled from the inner pocket of his jacket an envelope of color snapshots. She studied the faces of Sabrina's parents, two uncles and three male cousins—Sabrina had no siblings—and asked if she could keep the photos. He declined, saying he'd borrowed them from Sabrina's album and didn't want to raise her suspicions should she find them missing.

"I know it's short notice," Andersen said as he replaced the pictures in his coat, "but I'm going down to Pebble Beach early tomorrow, Saturday, on business and staying overnight. Are you available to come with me?"

Lauren made a pretense of checking the appointment book on her desk. "No, I don't have anything planned for this weekend. That would be fine. I'll give you my home address and you can pick me up there." She wondered briefly how they would work out the sleeping arrangements, but he'd probably rent a suite with a fold-out couch.

As they emerged from her offices into the hall, a lurking figure caught Lauren's eye. It was Bill Donelan, the rival private investigator who had recently taken the office next to hers. Lauren shook her client's outstretched hand. "Thank you for coming in, Mr. Andersen."

"No, thank *you*." Perfect white teeth flashed her an engaging smile. "And please, since we'll be working together, call me Nat."

"I'm Lauren."

He let go of her hand. "I'll see you tomorrow then, about seven."

She watched him walk the short distance to the elevator. He glanced only briefly at the tall man in the brown tweed sports coat and tie who stood outside one of the office doors thumbing through his mail. Nat turned and gave her a final wave, but she didn't go back into her office.

Lauren and her secretary had seen Donelan in the hall several times before, and he usually had a cigarette in his hand. The suite he'd rented next to hers was small—only a reception area and one office. Her father had used the rooms for his personal office and a file-storage area; with the downscaling of the agency,

Lauren had been forced to give up the lease on the space.

When encountering Donelan smoking in the corridor, she'd always assumed he didn't want to smell up his quarters. But now that she thought about it, she'd never actually seen his cigarette burning. It was always dangling from his fingers as though he was just about to light up when she appeared.

Suspicion crept into Lauren's mind. Maybe it was time to ask her new neighbor a few pointed questions. She shot her cuffs beneath the jacket of her wool pantsuit and stepped forward.

Donelan glanced up from the stack of envelopes in his large hands. As she approached, his umber-colored eyes turned wolfishly dark, and his slow smile struck her more like a proposition than a greeting. The roguish scar on his right cheek only added to the impression.

Lauren's mouth twisted into an automatic frown, born from too many years of men, who were strangers, whistling and casting unwanted "compliments."

Until now, she'd been favorably impressed with Bill Donelan. The man had a rough, well-muscled look that was appealing. There was a rawness and a toughness about him, as though he spent a lot of time outdoors in the sun and the wind. It was easy to picture him stalking through the forest with a deer rifle slung over one shoulder or squatting on the ground as he expertly ignited a camp fire with flint and steel. But it had been a long time since Lauren found the look of desire in a man's eyes flattering.

BILL DONELAN gave himself the pleasure of studying his colleague as she approached. He was an old film buff, and like the movie queens of his youth, Lauren Pierce was utterly fascinating. She was perfect—classically beautiful and elegant—and had a way of moving and dressing that told the world she was a quality woman. Those slightly tilted aqua eyes beneath the sculpted brows and thick lashes were smoldering and sexy as hell. It was like seeing Grace Kelly come alive again—Lauren's willowy figure and full breasts reminded him of the princess's. But she wore her chestnut hair differently, swept back off her forehead and held back in a French twist. And her face was really more like Kim Novak's, in *Vertigo*, wasn't it? Yes, definitely.

When she stopped in front of him, one delicate brow arched, he realized he'd been staring and broke off his gaze. No need to forget his manners, just because Lauren Pierce was gorgeous enough to stop traffic on Santa Rosa Avenue.

"HOW ARE YOU doing?" Donelan asked her, breaking off his insulting gaze and turning his body to lean casually back against the wall. At least now he was closer to eye level with her, Lauren thought. The giant must be six foot six!

"Good morning," she said crisply. "I'm fine. How's business?"

He turned his head to eye her again and shrugged one broad shoulder. "It's slow. But you know how it is. I didn't expect people to come beating down my door right away." He changed the subject. "That man who just left looked familiar. Isn't he Nathaniel Andersen, the computer manufacturer?"

Lauren's mind clicked, and she remembered where she'd seen Andersen's name before. In the *Press Democrat* a few days ago she'd read a front-page story about Micom, Inc., based in Santa Rosa.

"His company just released that new computer voice processor, didn't they?" Bill asked. "The one that can take human dictation and turn it into printed copy at the rate of 120 words a minute?"

Lauren almost nodded. The newspaper had called it a major technological advance, one that would make millions for Micom and put its owner, Nathaniel Andersen, in the history books.

Remembering Nat's need for privacy, she said, "I'd rather not say who he was."

"Nice client to have," Bill said. The corner of his mouth quirked up with what might have been admiration, or envy.

"Mmm." Lauren's eyes narrowed. "Speaking of business, is this your first . . . independent agency?"

"Yes." He kept his weight on the wall but leaned toward her. "Actually I'm running a branch of my uncle's P.I. office, which is based in Los Angeles."

Lauren grimaced. If Donelan's confident smile was designed to disarm her, he wasn't fooling her one bit. *Oh, brother,* she muttered to herself. Donelan probably wasn't licensed as a private investigator and was trying to slide by, working under his uncle's license long-range—a definite no-no.

"You stand around in this hallway a lot," she observed. "Aren't you afraid your phone will ring and you'll miss it?"

He frowned slightly and straightened up, like a lion rousing itself at a strange scent in the wind. "No, if the phone rings, I can always run in and get it."

Lauren's eyes fell to his stack of mail. The top envelope bore the return address of the Private Investigation Correspondence Schools of America. She took a deep breath. "Is that your alma mater?"

He glanced down at the envelope and snorted—*she must be making a joke.* "This?" He held up the envelope. "It's just junk mail. You probably get them, too."

"No." Lauren crossed her arms. "I don't get mail like that, because I've never had anything to *do* with places like that. You see, I apprenticed with my father during the summers while I was in college and for three years full-time before I earned my license, and now that my father is gone, I'm the owner of Pierce Investigations." The man was frowning fiercely at her, and she found she had to swallow before continuing. "Donelan, I'm not sure what your background is or what your intentions are, but I suspect you've been loitering here in the hallway, hoping to waylay a potential client who might be looking for *my* office, not *yours.*"

"That's ridiculous!"

"Then why are you always hanging around out here?"

Rather than answering her, he stared back, his mouth set in a mulish line.

His stonewalling made her angrier. "And why haven't you put your name on the door?" She jabbed a finger at the black lettering on the frosted glass. It read simply Private Investigator. "Anyone coming out of the elevator or up the stairs looking for Pierce Investigations would pass here first and could easily mistake your office for mine!"

As she spoke, the scar on Donelan's cheek began to turn an ominous red. "Look," he growled. He advanced on her so that their bodies almost touched, and she had to keep herself from flinching as the full force and heat of his masculine presence suddenly bore down on her. "If anyone ever stepped into my office looking for you, I wouldn't think twice about sending them over. But if the sign on the door bugs you—" he gestured curtly with his head "—as a professional courtesy, I'll put my name up there."

"See that you do," Lauren said, then finally allowed herself to step back. She swiveled quickly on her heel and marched toward her office.

The sense of his eyes burning into her back made her want to scrunch her shoulders, but she kept them rigid. Watch it, she told herself, forcing down her unease. She'd spoken her mind and succeeded in getting him to agree to identify his office. Since she'd won, there was no reason to feel he'd gotten the better of her.

Donelan called out a brusque command for her to come back. To steel herself, she concentrated on re-stirring her anger. As if her business wasn't bad enough, this upstart from a correspondence school had to come along with designs on stealing her clients. And the office where he'd planted his disreputable behind was the very one where her father had sat! It was all too much.

Donelan's voice compelled her to hesitate a moment at her door before her determination resolidified. She didn't look back.

"Good day, Donelan!"

Chapter Two

Two days later, Lauren stood in the ladies' lounge of the Inn at Spanish Bay, leaning toward the mirror to apply fresh lipstick. She and Nat had just finished a relaxed breakfast in the hotel dining room, reading the Sunday paper as they ate, and would be heading back to Santa Rosa in a few minutes.

It was a four-hour drive from Pebble Beach to home. They'd taken the inland highway the day before, when they'd driven down in Nat's chauffeured Mercedes limousine. Today Nat had promised they'd take the coastal route back, and Lauren was looking forward to some spectacular scenery.

She smiled to herself as she patted a stray hair back into her bun. Thank goodness she hadn't been swayed by her misgivings and refused this job! Staying at the world-class resort in the opulent two-bedroom suite Nat rented had been an adventure. Too bad more of her clients weren't this wealthy!

Yesterday had passed uneventfully. They'd spent most of the afternoon on the Pebble Beach Golf Course, Lauren watching as Nat played with two

Japanese business associates. She'd had Nat's chauffeur and acting caddy, Dirk DiMucci, as her companion in the golf cart. Dirk was a dark-complexioned native Italian with a thick accent, wiry build and sharp features. She'd tried to engage him in conversation, but when he made it clear he was more interested in catching smokes at the green, and furtively glancing about the fairways, she gave up and spent her time studying the craggy coastline through the cypress trees.

The game had been followed by an hour or so of business discussion in Nat's suite, then the Japanese had left to catch a late flight back to Tokyo. The dinner she and Nat shared in the public dining room was a quiet one.

Looking back on it this morning as she prepared for the drive home, she reflected that Nat Andersen was very unlike most of the men she met socially. He hadn't eyed her lasciviously, tried to turn the conversation to personal matters, made sexual innuendos or otherwise caused her to feel uncomfortable. On the contrary, he'd been consistently thoughtful and respectful. For that, she was grateful. In fact, if the man hadn't been so totally absorbed in his work and if he'd possessed more of a sense of humor, along with a divorce decree, she might have been interested in him as more than a client.

As Lauren reentered the lobby, she spotted Nat by the bell station, talking with someone.

The other man was squat and heavyset, his salt-and-pepper hair thinning to baldness, and he wore the familiar attire of the resort: baggy slacks and a golfing sweater.

She couldn't see their faces with their backs turned to her, but a certain stiffness in the two men's postures warned her something was wrong. She tried to catch what they were saying, but a phone at the front desk began to ring, and an elderly couple, apparently hard-of-hearing, shouted at each other as they passed her on their way to the restaurant.

As she came up closer, the heavyset man raised a finger and jabbed it at Nat. There was no mistaking his words at this range. "You've gone too far, Andersen," he growled. "You're going to regret this."

Before Nat could respond, the man broke off and brushed angrily past Lauren.

Lauren felt the old familiar thrill go up her back—half warning, half call to a challenge. She reached out to touch Nat's arm; he seemed frozen in place as he watched the retreating man.

"Who was *that?*"

"You heard him?"

"Just his parting shot. Not a fan of yours, I take it."

"No." He tucked his bottom lip between his teeth. After a moment he said, "But there's no going back now," speaking more to himself than Lauren. He put his hand on her back and steered her toward the hotel entrance. As they walked out, he leaned down to speak in her ear. "My guess is it won't be long now before Sabrina hears about my 'affair' with you. That was Chuck Caine—he's an old friend of the Falletti family and a kind of older-brother figure to Sabrina. He spotted us going up to the suite last night and again this morning at breakfast.''

''Where does he live?''

''In Rohnert Park.''

Just south of Santa Rosa, Lauren thought. She had already memorized the short, powerfully built figure and the injured, resentful brown eyes above the thick mustache.

''Is he, was he, a friend of yours, too?'' she asked as they emerged into the cool, fog-shrouded air.

Nat raised one arm and motioned for Dirk to bring the limousine up. ''No, we're not particular friends, and Caine has a temper to rival that of Sabrina's father and cousins. I don't want to exaggerate, Lauren, but I'd like you to keep a careful eye out for him. If we run into him again, he's liable to try using more than words to chastise me.''

LAUREN SAT in her office Monday morning, a brooding frown on her face. Upon returning from Pebble Beach the day before, she'd decided it would be prudent to get some backup on this case—someone to follow her and Nat Andersen on their next ''date'' and keep an eye out for Sabrina's supporters in case they showed up.

But the investigator who had worked for her and her father had found a job with another agency in San Francisco shortly after Lauren was forced to let him go, and of the two free-lance investigators she sometimes hired, one was out of town and the other was laid up with a broken leg. There were only six other agencies in Sonoma County, ten fewer than there'd been before the recession. She'd just spoken to the last of them on the phone, and all were too busy with their own cases to lend her a hand.

Not only couldn't she find the help she needed, she felt like the only P.I. in Sonoma County who wasn't fully employed! *It's just a coincidence that they've all got jobs at the moment,* she told herself. *You're not being passed over. You're not a failure.* Still, the thought that she might be seen to have some kind of leprosy flitted through her mind.

She leaned back in her chair and brought her pen to her lips. Nat was a good client, and a nice guy. He deserved the best service she could give him, which was a two-person team.

She swiveled in her chair to stare through the blind at the busy shops along Fourth Street. She hated being forced to consider him, but it was clear that Bill Donelan was the only gumshoe in town who was available.

She bet she could get him cheap, though, trying to console herself with the thought. He probably wasn't licensed, but that wouldn't matter if he was working under her license. At least he was a warm body, with eyes and ears. She shuddered at the unprofessionalism of that particular rationalization!

But what alternative did she really have? None.

BILL LOOKED UP from his desk at the sound of the outer door opening. It was Julie, the secretary from next door. Seeing her reminded him instantly of his run-in with Ms. Lauren Pierce last Friday.

It had been a hell of a wrong foot to get off on with the first colleague he'd made serious contact with here in Santa Rosa! The whole episode was so absurd that, looking back on it now, he wondered if he'd imagined it.

He'd tried his best to hold his tongue, but Lauren had made it very difficult. If she'd asked him civilly, he would have told her he was just stretching his legs and getting a breath of air before returning to his cramped office. Jeez, that should have been obvious! But instead, she'd jumped on him like a screaming banshee.

Mistaking him for some inexperienced fly-by-night...that was rich! Talk about harebrained. Now that the initial flush of anger had passed, he actually found the episode rather amusing. He'd probably just been in the wrong place at the wrong time. The woman already had some other bee in her bonnet when she came upon him. One way or another, though, it *was* a shame, not only because they were neighbors and stuck right next to each other, but also because he'd been looking forward to asking her out to dinner as soon as the timing seemed right.

Lauren's middle-aged secretary crossed the empty reception area and paused in the door.

"Morning, Julie," Bill greeted her. He grinned. "Run out of creamer again?"

"No, thanks awfully. I picked up a jar last week." Her slight British accent made the words sound pleasantly crisp. She smiled and pushed her glasses up on her thin nose. "Lauren would like a word, if you've the time."

Bill hid his surprise. "Did she say what she wants?"

"No, she just asked if you'd step over."

It sounded as though Ms. Pierce wanted to apologize. His lips pulled back like a crocodile's as he rose and grabbed his sport coat from the back of his chair. "Well, let's not keep the lady waiting."

LAUREN NODDED at Bill's greeting and motioned him to the chair across from her desk.

As Donelan unbuttoned his jacket and sat down, for a moment, Lauren was reminded strongly of her father. How strange! Donelan was about a head and a half taller than Lawrence Pierce had been, hard and muscular where her father had been paunchy. And Bill was charged with a raw, vaguely disturbing virility that her father had never had. So why had she thought of Dad? She knew Donelan, a rank amateur, wasn't in the same league as her father, but still, seeing him here, she felt oddly reassured about this case that looked as though it might turn dangerous.

"Thanks for coming over," she said, smiling more warmly than she'd planned to.

"No trouble at all," Bill drawled, the deep timbre of his voice pleasing her ears.

Lauren reminded herself to keep her guard up. He looked calm and relaxed, but she bet he was curious as hell to know why she wanted to see him.

"I need someone to do some surveillance work, but the situation is a bit unusual," she began. It was the first time she'd had to explain the case to an outsider—the conversation had never gotten this far with the other agencies she'd called. She'd confided in Julie, but her secretary knew her and had a respect for her that was unshakable. Lauren didn't want Bill to think she was a high-priced call girl—better to emphasize that she was protecting Andersen.

"My client is a man seeking a divorce," she said carefully. "The wife's family members are apparently notorious for their hot tempers and hair-trigger reactions, and I've been hired to make sure they don't do some violence to the client before they calm down and accept the inevitability of the divorce."

Bill struggled to keep a straight face; Lauren Pierce was undoubtedly the most beautiful bodyguard he'd ever seen. With the proper air of gravity he asked, "You've been working the case alone?"

"Yes." She hurried on, "I'd like someone to ride shotgun, to make sure one of the family or friends doesn't take us unawares while I'm with the client. Do you think you can do it?"

Bill nodded sagely, his mind flicking over the thousands of hours of surveillance work he'd done. He spread his palms upward. "No problem."

Lauren took a moment to feel impressed with Bill's nonchalance. He certainly didn't lack self-confidence. Well, that was good. A P.I. needed to be part actor.

"Do you have photos?" Bill asked.

"No, but I can give you a list of names, and the newspaper morgue will have pictures of all of them. The, ah—" she cleared her throat "—client is Nat Andersen, and the wife's family are the Fallettis of Sonoma."

Bill didn't bat an eyelash. "The wine-making Fallettis?"

"Yes." For some reason, his steady gaze was making it difficult for her to think. He was wearing only a moderate amount of after-shave, yet the spicy aroma seemed to have expanded to fill the room. "There's the father, two uncles, three cousins and an old family friend, Chuck Caine," she said, willing herself to concentrate so she could recall the list. "By the way, Caine caught Nat and I together down in Pebble Beach yesterday, and he was angry enough to threaten Nat. You'll have to look at the photos today and be ready to follow us this evening. I'm accompanying Nat to an early supper at five-thirty."

"I can be back here by four."

"That's fine. Nat's picking me up at the corner of Fourth and D. I assume you have a car that's not conspicuous?"

"Yes, regulation blue. Not too clean, not too dirty."

She rose, suddenly eager to conclude the interview and open her window. Looking Bill in the face made her uncomfortable, so her eyes strayed downward. His neck was thick and straight, the red silk tie knotted neatly beneath the slight bulge of his Adam's apple. As he leaned forward, his shoulders and biceps strained the seams of his gray tweed jacket. And his chest beneath the starched white shirt was so broad it obscured the chair back.

"I think you should know something about me if we're going to work together," he was saying. "As for my experience—"

Lauren snapped back to reality, angry and embarrassed that she'd allowed her mind to wander all over her new employee. "Don't tell me!" She threw up her hands and silenced him. "I don't want to know." She busied herself straightening the Andersen file on the desk. "As for compensation, how does fifteen dollars an hour sound, plus expenses?"

Bill's mouth clamped shut, his initial surprise and pleasure at her offer destroyed. He almost told her to forget it and find someone else, but practicality caught the rebuff as it was leaving his throat. He'd spent the last week making contacts in Sonoma County, paying visits to insurance companies, lawyers, the risk-management directors of local governments and others who might need the services of a private investigator. He knew that with time these introductions would pay off, but so far his phone hadn't jingled. It would feel good to get a break from the PR and do some real work again. Besides, hiring him to sit and watch Lauren all evening was like paying him to watch Marilyn Monroe movies. The thought made him chuckle.

"Did I say something funny?" Lauren asked, her brow creased in bewilderment.

"No, not at all. I accept your offer, and I'll get right on it."

BILL PLANTED HIMSELF in Lauren's doorway a few minutes after five that afternoon and waited while she copied the computer file she was working with on to a floppy diskette.

Lauren looked up at the man who filled her doorway; he was leaning casually against the jamb, his right leg crossed over the left, the toe of his brown wing tip dug into the carpet. For some reason, despite his coat and tie, Lauren felt as if she was gazing into the eyes of a young Matt Dillon. She could easily imagine him in a dusty pair of chaps and leather vest, a Stetson pushed back on his broad forehead. The scar on his cheek added to the image of a cowboy just off the range, checking out the action from the boardwalk of Dodge City.

The marshal cut a grin, and Lauren's cheeks reddened as she quickly turned back to her computer. "I'm just finishing up here." She pulled the diskette from the drive and replaced it in a file tray. "Did you find the photos?"

"Yes."

She chose that moment to stand up, and it was Bill's turn to lose his train of thought. He'd never seen the female P.I. dressed as she was. She had on a very short black skirt and dark stockings that revealed every luscious curve of her buttocks and shapely legs. A gold lamé belt encircled her tiny waist, and the fuzzy sweater she wore made her full breasts look even more enticing. Gad, how he'd love to run his hands over that angora, hear Lauren's encouraging moan, slip his hands underneath and over her warm flesh....

"All of them?" Lauren asked a little impatiently.

"What? Oh yes, the photos." Bill shook the fantasy from his head. "They were all there."

Lauren regarded him sourly, and he realized that, though her once-over had flattered him, she was offended by his attraction to her. It was plain she wanted to be treated like one of the boys, but at the same time she gave off an aura of repressed sexuality he found maddening. He could sense it in her pouty lips, the way her hips swayed as she came around from behind her desk. But she did have every right to keep things businesslike. Until she gave him some go-ahead sign, he decided, he would have to treat her like a fellow detective and nothing more.

He stepped forward to help her on with her coat, and his eyes automatically registered the provocative arch of her shoulder blades beneath the sweater. He stopped himself with a rueful frown. Pretending not to be attracted to her was going to prove a tougher assignment than the surveillance!

He composed his face in a careful mask as Lauren turned to face him.

"This is an important case," she said. The corners of her mouth turned down. "I want you to warn us the moment you see any of the relatives enter the restaurant."

"Hopefully it won't happen."

"But if it does, that's what I'm paying you for."

Bill bit back a retort as she led the way. "Don't worry. I even hunted down a picture of Sabrina Andersen, though she wasn't on your list. She's a very attractive woman." He added a short, admiring whistle for emphasis.

Lauren glanced at him over her shoulder, her brows raised like bird wings.

"Don't you agree?" he asked.

"I haven't seen her picture," Lauren admitted reluctantly. She busied herself with locking the door and dismissed the pinprick of jealousy she'd felt, telling herself she was merely annoyed she'd been lax in her homework. "Sabrina's wasn't among the pictures Nat showed me," she said, "but then, I don't expect I'll ever run into her—she's very reclusive."

"Mmm," Bill answered noncommittally. They started down the hall side by side. "While I was at the *Press Democrat,* I took the opportunity to do a little background research on the subjects. Quite a successful group. The Fallettis established their wine-making empire in the late thirties. Chuck Caine keeps a low profile, but he's still one of the top men in the computer industry."

As the elevator doors opened, Lauren suddenly remembered she'd forgotten to turn off the coffee-maker. How annoying! Why did she allow herself to be so easily distracted today? "I've got to go back to the office for a minute. I'll meet you in the lobby," she said.

By the time she secured her office again, her watch said five-twenty, and she did *not* want to be late to meet her client. Rather than waiting for the ancient, poky elevator, she took the stairs.

As she emerged into the lobby, Bill and the maintenance man, Skip, chuckled together before the opened glass door of the building directory. Their backs were to her, and they didn't hear her.

"That lady detective sure is a looker," Skip crowed. "Her old man had a face like a bulldog. He was a great guy, but I sure never knew how he fathered a daughter like that." He drew a long breath and let it out. "Face like an angel and a body made for *Playboy*."

"You've got that right, brother," the P.I. said.

Lauren couldn't see Bill's face, but she bet he was grinning like a demon.

"She's probably even sexier when she's mad," the janitor kidded.

"She'd blow up if she saw you switch her office number to mine, but I'll admit it's a great idea." Bill slapped the other man's back and laughed heartily.

Lauren pushed the stairwell door closed and it clanged behind her.

"What are you doing?" she demanded in a low voice, stalking up to them, hands in rigid fists at her side.

Skip looked startled, as though he'd been caught peeing in the bushes. Bill's eyes flashed ceilingward, but his hands came to rest on his hips in a John Wayne pose.

"We weren't doing nothing, Miss Pierce," the janitor said in a nervous voice. "Just updating the board for that new lawyer who moved in on the third floor." He hastily turned back to his job.

"We were just joking around, Lauren," Bill said. He dipped his head a moment. "I'm sorry if you overheard."

Lauren tried to stare him down like an angry drill sergeant. When he looked regretful but didn't flinch, she gave up and barked, "Come on, we're late!"

Bill let her brush past him and smiled as she tried to effect a powerful stride in her three-inch spike heels. She beat him to the entrance and flung the door open so that he barely missed being hit. Her look of disappointment, when she saw he'd escaped, was so acute he chuckled. The woman certainly had fire!

"I warn you, Donelan!" Lauren's ankle turned under slightly as they hit the sidewalk; her already flushed face turned redder, but she kept going. "I warn you. I have a brown belt in karate. If you wish to remain employed by me, much less in one piece, put all thought of another stunt like switching our office numbers out of your head."

The response, "Yes, sir!" flew to Bill's lips, but he told himself he'd better behave. Skip was right; though Bill had thought it impossible, Lauren *was* even sexier when she was mad.

Bill split off to get his car and Nat's limousine was just entering the intersection as Lauren hurried up. Dirk double-parked and jumped out to open the door for her.

"How are you?" Nat greeted her from the car's darkened interior. "You look very nice tonight."

"Thank you," she said, giving him a grateful smile as she felt the compliment soothe her ruffled ego. Remembering her duty, she twisted in the seat to look out the back; a blue Ford Taurus sedan with Bill at the wheel pulled up behind them.

She was about to tell Nat about hiring Donelan, when he reached for the cellular phone. "Excuse me, but there's a call I have to make."

THE FIVE-STAR Vineyard Restaurant was on the very outskirts of Santa Rosa, almost into the country.

As they waited for the maître d' to seat them, Lauren noted that Nat seemed stiffer, less at ease than he had on their first date. He was probably nervous that closer to home they might accidentally meet one of the Fallettis. Nevertheless, he was paying her to put on a good act, and she didn't want to take his money for nothing.

"Why don't you put your arm around my waist," she whispered.

"Huh?"

"Try to loosen up a bit. Pretend you're attracted to me."

Nat gave her a nervous smile as his arm tentatively circled her. "You're right of course."

They were shown to a table near the windows in the quietest part of the two-room dining area. The sun had already set, and a vineyard beyond the restaurant was illuminated with silvery moonlight. Lauren reflected that, under other circumstances, with a different escort, this evening could have been wonderfully romantic.

The waiter was with them in a thrice; Nat ordered a martini; Lauren asked for a ginger ale, since she was officially on duty.

She saw Bill enter the dining room, then lost track of him as Nat said something to her. She leaned intimately toward him as they discussed the menu and Nat reciprocated, finally warming to his part. He said something funny and she clasped his hand on the table for a moment, laughing as though she found him really amusing.

They had just finished ordering when the headwaiter came up to their table with a cordless phone in his hand. "Mr. Andersen?"

Nat nodded.

"A call for you from Mr. Mark Andersen."

Nat pursed his lips as the waiter handed him the phone, and Lauren guessed he might want some privacy while he took the call. She'd been looking for a reason to get away from the table, anyway.

As she headed in the direction of the ladies' room, her eyes covertly scanned the busy dining room for sight of Bill Donelan. She finally spotted him against the far wall and headed for his table.

Despite the fact that he'd apologized, she still felt angry at the remarks he'd shared with the maintenance man in the foyer of their office building. "What are you doing sitting way over here?" she demanded.

Bill's lips pulled back. "Don't get your dander up." The grasp he put on her wrist was light but forceful as he pushed her down into a chair. "Have a seat. People will stare." When she glowered at him, he whispered, "Be glad I'm not even farther away. For an expensive restaurant, the maître d' is unusually resistant to bribery."

Lauren looked doubtful. "Can you really see us from here?"

"Yes, I can see you and your little friend just fine!"

Considering how tall he was, Lauren decided he probably *could* see over the other diners with no trouble.

"Nat's a client, not a friend." She still felt hot and bothered but wasn't sure if it was at Bill or at herself for making a big to-do over nothing. She pushed herself away from the table and said, "I'll see you later."

By the time Lauren returned to their table, Nat wore a scowl on his face and appeared deep in thought.

Lauren slid in across from him. "Is everything all right?"

Nat stared at her a moment as though uncertain how to answer her question. "Oh, yes, fine. That was my brother, Mark, on the phone. He's flying in tomorrow and didn't trust me to remember to pick him up at the airport." He gave a snort. "I told him he could have left a message with my butler, but he doesn't trust servants."

"Does your brother live in Santa Rosa?"

"No, Seattle. He's just coming for a visit. Ah, here's our first course. I skipped lunch today and I'm famished."

Their meal of rack of lamb was delicious. Their main topic of conversation while they ate was food and other restaurants they'd been to.

The main course was winding down when Lauren noticed a woman in a plain navy-colored shift drifting among the tables. She had black hair that fell straight and limp to her waist, and Lauren unconsciously noted how the oversize chemise hung like a sack on her thin frame. A bit underdressed for this place, a part of Lauren's mind registered as she returned her attention to what Nat was saying.

A few minutes later, the straggly woman approached their table. Lauren expected her to pass by, but she stopped, standing like a post between Lauren and Nat.

Nat's breath sucked in as he looked up from his plate. "Sabrina!"

Chapter Three

The woman's face was nearly vacant; she stared at Nat as though looking right through him, then slowly turned her head to gaze at Lauren for a long moment.

Lauren felt like a criminal.

Nat's lips parted, but the power of speech had left him. It was Sabrina who spoke. "She's very pretty, Nat. You have good taste, better taste than when you married me." Her voice, an odd monotone, was almost eerie. "Maybe that's my problem." She gave a dry little laugh, like leaves in the wind, and Lauren shuddered.

Nat made a strangled sound in his throat, but Sabrina didn't notice. Her gaze wandered to some undefined point over their heads as she said, "I'm not feeling well. I think I'll go…home." Her eyes floated back to Lauren and became hard and focused. "He can have a divorce if he wants it," she said flatly. "But you'll live to regret this, both of you."

Like a dark ghost, Sabrina Andersen turned and drifted out of the dining room.

It took Nat a minute to regain his composure as Lauren studied the tablecloth. The waiter came to remove their plates, and Nat asked him to hold off serving the coffee and dessert.

"I'm very sorry about this, Lauren," Nat said, finding his tongue. "I never expected to see Sabrina here. She doesn't go out much, except to her doctor's office. I really didn't want her to find out this way." When Lauren didn't look up, he added, "I realize this must be terribly embarrassing for you."

Lauren pasted on her cool professional smile before raising her chin. "Well, it was unexpected, but in my line of work, you can't always predict what'll happen."

His facial muscles relaxed a fraction. "Thanks, Lauren. You're very understanding." He leaned back in the chair and his knuckles played against his lips as he thought aloud. "Sabrina doesn't usually go out without me. But our butler knew where I was dining. I suppose she could have gotten an unexpected urge to join me."

Lauren thought that an unlikely possibility. "Do you think Chuck Caine told her about us?"

"Caine?" His brow creased. "No. Well, maybe. He could have passed the word to one of her male relatives. I just didn't expect her to confront me herself." He straightened. "Would you like some dessert, or shall we just get out of here?"

"No, I'm fine, we can leave."

Nat twisted in his chair to summon the waiter, and Lauren cast a withering glance in the direction of Bill

Donelan, who had anticipated their departure and was hastily paying his bill. Bill knew what Sabrina Andersen looked like; he'd almost bragged about digging up her photo. Sabrina must have entered the dining room a good few minutes before arriving at Nat's table. Bill should have warned them she was coming!

Nat was silent on the ride back to Lauren's. He put some soothing Windham Hill instrumental music on the stereo, then became lost in brooding contemplation. When the chauffeur pulled the car up in front of Lauren's condominium, Nat said, "I'll see you to your door."

As they walked the few yards to her unit, Lauren tried to sound neutral, if not cheerful. "It looks like you won't be needing my services anymore."

"I guess you're right."

He sounded so deflated she wondered if the events of the evening had changed his mind about wanting a divorce. Perhaps though he no longer loved Sabrina, he was still very fond of her. After eight years of marriage it wasn't surprising he should feel strange, even sad, at the thought of leaving her. Still, Sabrina had been so spacey, so creepy. Lauren couldn't imagine being chained to such a partner for life.

As Lauren reached into her evening bag for her keys, she wondered what Nat would have to face when he returned home. Would Sabrina be waiting to accuse him, eager to make a scene, or would she be deep in some drug-induced sleep? Either way, Lauren felt sorry for Nat.

As she turned the key in the lock, empathy made her say, "Would you like to come in for a nightcap—to close our business relationship?"

As they shared a glass of wine on the living room sofa, he told her he'd send her a check "with something extra in it," since she had done such a professional job and the assignment had turned out to be shorter than expected. Lauren told him there was no need, but he insisted. A few minutes later, Nat set his glass down on the coffee table. "I'd better get going, make sure Sabrina got home all right. She has her own car, but she's hardly used it in years."

As they said good-night on the front steps, Lauren's mothering instincts couldn't stand it; she impulsively reached up and gave his hunched shoulders a hug, then squeezed his upper arms. "Good luck."

"Thanks, Lauren." He bent down and, to her surprise, kissed her on the lips, then turned and walked to the curb where his car waited. Dirk, the chauffeur, ground out a cigarette on the pavement, then frowned sullenly as he reached down to open the door for his employer. *There's an unhappy young man,* Lauren thought. She'd never heard him speak to Nat except to say, "Yes, sir."

The gray limousine slid away from the curb, and a blue sedan flashed by, going too fast, in the opposite direction. She'd almost forgotten about Bill Donelan's surveillance!

AS LAUREN DROVE to work the next morning, she thought about Donelan. She'd been disappointed in his performance last night, but she'd known she was taking a chance when she hired him. He was just starting out in the private-investigation business, so she couldn't really blame him. Something told her Donelan would quickly grow out of the rookie stage—if he could stay in business long enough to learn! As she walked from the parking structure to her office, she decided to be generous, not make a big deal about last night and quietly cut him a check as soon as Nat paid her.

When she emerged from the elevator, she was surprised to see Bill Donelan waiting for her outside her office, leaning against the door in what was becoming a characteristic pose. For a moment, the thought that they'd probably never work together, or spar together, again made her feel mildly depressed.

"Good morning," she said as she approached.

Bill just grunted.

She noticed that his features had a sour cast to them this morning. Perhaps he felt badly about last night. She unlocked the door and Bill silently followed her into the still, chilly office. Why was he in such a hurry to see her? she wondered.

"Well, I guess I can close the file on this one," she said as she dropped her purse into the lower drawer of her desk. Bill carried nothing in his hands, so she said, "I'll pay you as soon as I get your report."

She sat down and noted that Bill's face resembled a squall on a Teton lake. He took a seat also, and pulled a notebook out of his inner sport coat pocket, then began reading off the time he started the surveillance the evening before.

"No, I mean your *written* report," Lauren interrupted.

When he just stared malevolently at her, a disturbing thought occurred to her. "You do know how to write a surveillance report, don't you?" she said hopefully.

"Hell, of course I do!" Bill exploded. "And what about you? Do you know *your* job? Are you familiar with the private investigator's code of ethics?"

Lauren's jaw dropped. "What do you mean?"

"You know what I'm talking about," he responded, his voice lowering to a sulky growl.

This was a new one! After enduring his teasing, she felt a little thrill of satisfaction. She'd never seen Donelan in a pout before. He was positively standing on his head over something. How nice!

"No, I *don't* know what you're talking about," Lauren said, mirth in her eyes. "Perhaps you would enlighten me."

"Have you forgotten that little tryst you had with our client last night, Ms. Pierce?"

Tryst? For a moment, Lauren was flummoxed. Then it came to her: Bill must have seen Nat giving her that brief kiss at the door and assumed the worst. She almost exclaimed that they were only in her place for ten minutes, hardly time for a tryst, but then it occurred to her *she* was the lead investigator. Why should she allow him to put *her* on the carpet?

"I did nothing unethical with Nat, and that's all I intend to say on the matter." Lauren folded her arms assertively, but she also rolled her chair back a little farther from him.

"Right," Bill scoffed. "Since when is it acceptable practice for bodyguards to hold hands with their charges and kiss them on the mouth? I did some checking on Mr. Andersen yesterday afternoon. Did you know he's still living with his wife? Did he tell you *that?*"

Lauren sighed. She'd forgotten she hadn't told Bill that she'd been hired to pose as Nat's girlfriend to give his wife grounds for divorce. But what was the point of confessing that now? He might not believe her, and if he did, he'd probably demand to know why she'd taken such a flaky assignment. She didn't want to be forced into telling him how bad off she was financially.

"Did you know Nat was still with his wife?" Bill persisted.

Lauren threw up her hands. "Yes, *yes*. I knew!"

The hard line of Bill's jaw suddenly went slack and his eyes widened. Clearly he hadn't expected her answer, and she used his stunned silence to collect her thoughts. This confrontation was getting out of hand; she needed to regain control. The uncomfortable thought occurred to her that he might spread stories about her around town, use what he thought of as her indiscretion to give her a bad name. It would be a dirty trick, one he didn't really seem capable of, but if he was anxious enough to improve his own business...

The agency had to come first, so she'd better play her own trump card.

"What about *your* performance last night?" she said, putting on a tough face. "We haven't discussed that yet. How could you have failed to spot Mrs. Andersen? She had to have been roving around the dining room for some minutes before she found us."

When Bill looked stubbornly unchastened, Lauren continued, "Mrs. Andersen is under a psychiatrist's care. She could have walked into that restaurant with a gun and shot her husband *and* me!" She knew that was probably an exaggeration, but it didn't matter. "You endangered both of us through your laxity."

Bill's jaw worked for a moment, then he said quietly, "You're right." His face went deadly somber. "I have to admit that was a royal screwup on my part, Lauren, and I take full responsibility. I should have done a better job for you, and I'm sorry."

Lauren blinked at his magnanimous apology. She'd been all set to argue over his denial. She hadn't expected him to own up so handsomely. Still, she thought sadly, what else *could* he say, when he'd clearly made such a big mistake and had no excuse for it?

The unforeseen twists in this conversation were making her feel oddly bereft, and silence only made it worse. She searched for something to say. "You're new at this and inexperienced, so it's understandable you'll make some mistakes. I hate to say it, but the P.I. business doesn't allow you many—it's no way to impress your clients."

Bill didn't seem to be listening. He'd shifted his gaze to the ceiling, his index finger rubbing his lower lip. He growled something to himself she didn't quite catch, something about watching the damn scenery instead of the wife.

It occurred to Lauren she was playing the part of the big sister while ignoring the fact that she herself hadn't even had the foresight to secure a photo of Sabrina. Who was she trying to kid?

She cleared her throat. "Anyway, as I said, this assignment is concluded. Mrs. Andersen seems reconciled to the divorce, so our services are no longer needed."

The outer door opened, and Lauren gratefully caught sight of Julie Cox. The secretary entered and called out a good-morning.

Lauren returned the greeting, then told Bill softly, "I'll cut you a check when I get your report. Thank you."

He stood up slowly and flapped out his jacket, then unexpectedly moved around the desk to stand beside her chair.

"Thanks for what?" he said wryly, extending his hand.

Smiling, she stood up and took his hand, which enfolded hers like a warm, rough glove.

His touch was so powerful, so masculine. Even in the midst of disgrace, he seemed self-possessed. How had he bungled such an easy assignment?

Her eyes traveled up his shirt to his chin, the scar on his tanned cheek, his hooded eyes, which were focused at some point over her head. The irises were a deep brown with lighter specks, like fallen autumn leaves. So serious. His lower lip was full and smooth. As she watched, the corners turned up just a fraction, making lines from mouth to nose. His gaze finally connected with hers, and the ironic smile deepened.

"Thanks for the job," he said, his voice low. "If you ever decide you can trust me again, Lauren, give me a call."

The pad of his thumb stroked a line of heat across her wrist as he let her hand go. She knew she couldn't afford to trust him, but she said, "I will." Anyone watching her countenance sag as Bill Donelan left her office would have sworn she meant it, too.

LAUREN DIDN'T SEE Bill the rest of that day. He didn't seem to be in his office Thursday morning, either. And it was just as well, she told herself. Their interview had left her with oddly mixed emotions she felt she'd be safer not examining. Much as the man compelled her physically, his performance on the job was erratic and unreliable, his background and experience highly questionable, and his motives for moving in next to her still unknown. The next time she needed to consult with another P.I., she'd be crazy to choose Bill Donelan. Better to bring someone in from Marin County or San Francisco. Allowing Bill to engage her in conversation, if she met him in the elevator or the hall, would probably encourage him and complicate matters, so it was best simply to avoid him. And difficult though it proved to be, she put him from her mind, as well.

She had set aside Thursday to go over the agency's computerized bookkeeping records in preparation for filing her yearly tax return. The work proved to be an efficient, if depressing, distraction. Income for the last quarter was even lower than she'd estimated, and the business's reserve account had dwindled to a few hundred dollars.

By midafternoon, the whole dreary picture had become apparent. Lauren leaned back in her chair and rapped her pencil on the edge of the desk. The last substantial job she'd had was in November, helping investigate a tanker-trailer spill in Santa Rosa for an oil company, and that was a one-shot deal—not likely to be any repeat business from that quarter. This was the driest period for business she'd ever known.

She called Julie in, and they went over the accounts together, racking their brains for some further way to economize. The ninety-minute session only confirmed what Lauren already knew—there was no fat left to cut except Julie's salary. Lauren herself was withdrawing as little as she could to pay the rent on the condo and keep food in her cupboards.

Julie was the first to say it aloud. "You don't have to keep me on, love." She tilted her head, and though her voice was calm, Lauren saw her pale lashes bat behind the oversize frames of her glasses. "I can pick up some temp jobs for a few months until business picks up again, then come back."

"No," Lauren said fiercely, shoving the printout aside. "You need a steady income—you've got a daughter to support. Before I let you go, I'll start selling my furniture, or, worse—" she grinned for Julie's benefit "—move in with my mother."

Julie protested for a minute, but Lauren remained adamant, and the secretary looked relieved. As Julie went back to her desk in the reception area, Lauren wondered if she should start making a garage-sale list.

She was in the file room later when she heard the outer office door open. Hope leapt in her it might be a drop-in client, but she didn't want to race out with a hungry look on her face. When she emerged a minute later, the caller had gone.

"Who was that?" she asked Julie, who was clearing her desk for the day.

"Bill Donelan. He left this." Julie held up a manila folder. "He said I could dead file it."

"It must be his report." Lauren stifled a phantom pain in her chest.

When she didn't reach for the folder, Julie said, "Should I just put it with the Andersen file?"

"Yes . . . no." Lauren pursed her lips with uncertainty. "I'd better take a look at it. I'll just do it before I go." *And then I can forget about the whole episode once and for all.* She took the folder. "Did he give you a bill with it?"

"No," Julie said pointedly. Lauren was pretty sure her divorced secretary had a crush on the handsome P.I. next door; Julie had been slightly disapproving when her boss quarreled with him.

Lauren shrugged. "It's just as well he's not anxious, since I don't have the money to pay him, anyway."

She said good-night to Julie and carried the folder into her office. The first thing she noticed was that he'd neatly typed the name of the client on the tab. She knew Bill didn't have a secretary, and she'd fully expected him to turn in a handwritten report. The fact that he'd taken the time and trouble to type it impressed her.

The pages were neatly divided into sections with separate underlined headings. She'd intended just to skip through it, but she found herself sitting down at her desk and reading the first paragraph, which recounted the information Lauren had given him on the assignment, and the next one, which detailed the facts he'd dug up on the Falletti family members. The following page chronicled Bill's surveillance, with the times and locations accurately noted.

"Very nice," she murmured. It was only a simple surveillance. Still, where had he learned to write a report like this? From that correspondence school? The report was as good, no—she had to be honest—better than the one she'd written herself.

There were more sheets in the folder. She turned over the last typewritten page to find a short stack of black-and-white and color photocopies and realized they were copies of the newspaper-morgue photos of the Falletti family. She flipped through them, absently registering the shots of faces she'd memorized during her initial interview with Nat, until she came to one that was unfamiliar.

It was a wedding shot of Nathaniel Andersen, standing trim in black tie and tails with a glass of champagne raised in his hand. She had no trouble recognizing her former client, but the radiant woman in the elaborate veil and satin gown who shared his toast was a stranger.

Lauren studied the girl's short, curly blond hair, the full rosy cheeks and laughing blue eyes. She hadn't realized Nat was married before. Then something about the mouth and the nose caught her eye and she gasped. This wasn't some woman she'd never seen. It was Sabrina!

The change was incredible. Sabrina looked as if she had lost twenty pounds since this photo was taken. She must have bleached her hair for the wedding, as well as perming it, since it was now down to her waist and jet black.

Lauren's next realization flew on the heels of the first. No wonder Bill hadn't recognized Mrs. Andersen in the restaurant! He'd been looking for a fair-haired cherub, not the dark-haired, sallow wraith Sabrina had become.

Lauren flung herself back in her chair, not breathing. So why hadn't Bill told her? She wouldn't have blamed him for not recognizing Sabrina immediately. Who could have?

Her brows bunched as she pondered the puzzle of Bill's silence. Had he been embarrassed about not recognizing Sabrina? Why should he have been, when it was perfectly understandable? No...no, it was more likely he just didn't want to make excuses. Yes, that was it! Admiration flared in her breast. It reminded her of her father. He'd always kept a little plaque on his desk with the famous quote The Buck Stops Here.

She returned from stowing the report in the file room, growing more curious by the minute about who exactly Bill Donelan was and where he'd learned his skills. She started to reach for the phone, then glanced at her watch. Almost five-thirty. Her contact in L.A. would probably have gone home for the day, and if not, she didn't want to keep him back. She would have to wait until tomorrow.

SOME THREE HOURS later, atop Santa Rosa's Hood Mountain, Nat Andersen descended the staircase of his custom-built home.

"Hinshaw!" he called brusquely.

"Here, sir," replied the butler, stepping from the shadow of the stairwell to look up at his employer.

"I'm ready," Nat said. He bounded across the entryway and reached for a small oil painting that hung by the front door. The frame swung aside on invisible hinges, revealing an electronic control panel. Nat hit one of the switches, and as he and the butler emerged from the house, one of the doors began to rise on the detached five-car garage.

"Would you like me to drive, sir?" the butler offered hesitantly as Nat paced quickly to the garage.

"No, I'll do it," Nat said, jerking up the hand that carried the spare set of keys he always kept in his bedroom.

A few moments later, the gray Mercedes limousine glided from the garage. Out of necessity, Nat maintained a moderate speed as he wound along the flat but twisting private drive. It was a moonless night, and lanterns on short pylons, spaced periodically along the length of the drive, lit their way through the deeply wooded property. Nat flipped down the visor over the driver's seat to touch a button, and the massive gates at the entrance to the estate swung open as they appeared in the car's headlights. Hinshaw flinched, but the car just made it through the narrow opening as Nat kept his foot on the accelerator.

With barely a pause to flick his head both ways, Nathaniel Andersen turned his car onto the steep narrow road that zigzagged down Hood Mountain.

LAUREN ROSE at her usual time Friday morning, six o'clock, and went for a jog. Afterward she showered and dressed, then sat down at the dining table with the newspaper to eat a solitary breakfast. Her younger sister, Suzie, who was living with her for a few months while she planned her wedding, was still in the shower.

Lauren dug into her juice and shredded wheat with banana before slipping the rubber band off the newspaper and unfolding it on the glass tabletop.

The headline struck her like the blow of a fist, and she almost dropped her half-raised coffee mug. Setting the cup down unsteadily, she grasped the paper with both hands and drew it closer.

"God, no," she moaned. Her eyes ran over the first paragraph, but it only confirmed the truth of the bold black headline:

Computer Magnate Andersen
in Fatal Car Crash

Chapter Four

Heart pounding, Lauren read that Nathaniel Andersen had been driving his Mercedes down Los Alamos Road on Hood Mountain just before nine the previous night when the car apparently went out of control and skidded over the embankment. The sheriff's department reported that a passenger, Thomas Hinshaw, butler on the Andersen estate, had been thrown from the vehicle and was taken to Santa Rosa Memorial Hospital in a coma.

The sheriff's deputy in charge at the accident scene gave two possible explanations for the crash: Andersen could have swerved to avoid hitting one of the many deer that roamed the mountain, or the limousine could have had a mechanical failure of some kind. There would, of course, be an investigation to determine the exact cause of the accident.

Suzie shuffled into the kitchen, dressed in a skirt and blouse and fluffy slippers. "Good morning," she said.

Lauren's eyes flicked up absently to register her sister's petite, bouncy figure, but she didn't return the greeting.

"Hey, Sis. Yoo-hoo. You okay?"

"Yes." Lauren roused herself. "You remember that client I told you about, Nathaniel Andersen?"

Suzie pushed her shoulder-length blond hair behind her ears. "Yes, I remember. The one whose wife walked in on you in the restaurant."

"That's him. He was killed last night in an auto accident."

"You're kidding!" Suzie grimaced as she took the paper from Lauren's hand and eased into a chair. "That's terrible." When she'd read most of the story, Suzie glanced over at Lauren's distressed face. "He was a nice man, huh?"

"Yes. Very considerate. Thoughtful. He could have made a pass at me the night I brought him back here for a drink, but he didn't."

Suzie nodded. "Since you usually end up in a wrestling match with guys, he must have made quite an impression."

Lauren nodded. "He did."

Suzie got up to pour herself a cup of coffee, but she glanced over her shoulder at Lauren as she did. When she returned to the table, her face was thoughtful. "You look kind of tired, Laur. Why don't you take the day off?"

"And do what?" Lauren asked skeptically. *I don't have any social life,* she thought, but kept it to herself.

"My wedding dress came in and I'm going to get it fitted this afternoon. I'd love for you to see it, especially since you were too busy with that tanker-spill case to help me pick it out." Suzie pulled a face; Lauren looked sheepish. "Besides—" Suzie grinned to show she was just ribbing her sister "—I bet it'll cheer you up."

There weren't any cases, so why not? She might as well enjoy herself while her business dwindled away, and the thought of spending a day with her sister was so comforting it was irresistible. Lauren smiled at Suzie affectionately. "You're right. I'm completely in the mood. Let's do it!"

They picked their mother up on the way. Outside the bridal shop, the three women were stopped by a window display of the most breathtaking dress Lauren had ever seen.

It was an off-the-shoulder affair that hugged the mannequin's body straight down to the narrow hem. Both the dress and the tightly fitted sleeves were covered in an exquisite lace. Attached at the back of the waist was a satin bow with a stiff fall that formed a long, glorious train.

Lauren would have given a sigh of love, but she didn't want to risk hurting Suzie's feelings. She needn't have worried.

"That's a gorgeous dress!" Suzie cried. "I've got too much padding in the wrong places, but it would be fabulous on someone with a figure like yours, Lauren."

Lauren had to admit her sister was right—she could just picture herself in that gown, the simple spray of netting and pearls attached behind her swept-up hair.

Her mother's dry voice intruded on the picture. "By the time Lauren chooses a husband, that dress'll be long out of style."

"Mother!" Suzie said. "Lauren just hasn't found the right man yet."

"And she never will if she doesn't get out and meet more people."

"I'm perfectly happy being single," Lauren said. It was her stock response, but today the words seemed to ring with even less conviction than they usually did.

Sister and mother sat in the dressing room while the saleswoman helped Suzie step into her dress. When the tiny buttons were all done up the back and the chiffon skirt fluffed out, the attendant stepped back.

Suzie's face shone. "What do you think?"

There were tears in Mrs. Pierce's eyes. "You're so beautiful, sweetheart. The most beautiful bride ever. Like a princess in a fairy tale."

"Mother's right," Lauren breathed. "That's exactly how you look." *And Allen is so handsome,* she thought. *And loving and intelligent and great at what he does, selling real estate, with a promising career.* Lauren jumped up to hug her sister. "I'm so happy for you," she said.

As she kissed Suzie's cheek, Lauren was stabbed by a shameful realization. Her happiness for her sister was mixed with another emotion. Envy.

THE NEXT MORNING Suzie left to go up to Tahoe for the weekend with Allen Rogers and his parents. Lauren spent a quiet weekend on her own working on her taxes.

The weather was overcast, and just before lunch Saturday, she threw down her pencil and surveyed her silent living room in the gray light.

She thought she'd gotten used to living alone in the years since she'd moved out of her folks' house, but with Suzie absent, the house felt unbearably lonely. And in another six weeks Suzie would be getting married and moving in with her husband. Lauren would truly be alone again. The thought depressed her as much as the dismal figures on the form in front of her, more than the news of Nat Andersen's death.

As she slumped there in a blue funk, the words Bill Donelan had spoken to her in parting floated into her mind. *If you ever decide you can trust me again, Lauren, give me a call.* She replayed the scene in her mind, remembering with a little thrill the way his fingers had almost caressed hers as they shook hands....

No, she was being silly. Bill hadn't meant anything by the gesture except goodwill. Ridiculous to remember it as anything more, to try to read something into it. Besides, the man was insufferable, wasn't he? It infuriated her how she could never get the better of him. But Lauren found herself smiling at the thought.

She told herself to stop thinking about Bill Donelan. Despite the fact he'd proven he was intelligent and had integrity and was conscientious about his work, he was just too overbearing and not her type at all.

But she found she couldn't stop thinking about him. Little pictures of him kept intruding into her thoughts, and each time, the gloom she was under was dispelled a bit. It was like popping a chocolate in her mouth. Very addictive! And as the weekend wore on and the recollections continued, unbidden, she began to see a few things she'd missed in the heat of the moment.

She began to suspect that Bill's anger at her kissing Nat was caused by jealousy; it was not some sort of reprimand about her professional behavior, as she'd first assumed. His mumbled words about watching the scenery in the restaurant came back to her and took on a new significance. He'd been seated far from the windows and any view. By the scenery, had he meant *her,* and that she had distracted him from watching for Sabrina?

As she put a frozen dinner into the microwave Sunday night, she realized she was no longer feeling sorry for herself. The thought that she'd gotten under Bill Donelan's skin made her want to smile, made her feel good.

As she ate her food, she told herself she was certainly changing in her old age. Jealous, possessive men had always annoyed her. But recalling Bill Donelan's livid features, she felt flattered and, well, rather triumphant. She knew she should have told him the truth about Nat from the beginning. However, it was almost worth it, just to have the memory of Bill's jealous face.

A plaintive meow at the kitchen door reminded her she'd forgotten to feed Noodles, the neighbor's cat, who was shut up in the Youngs' garage, adjacent to her kitchen. It was a chore she'd been doing for the past week while the Youngs were away on vacation.

Lauren went outside and rested the plate of Cat Chow on the Youngs' barbecue while she opened the unlocked garage door.

"Don't you dare trip me," Lauren warned the tabby, then hesitated a moment before entering the dark garage. The light switch was behind a heavy mattress set, so she never bothered with it, but the darkness always made her feel uneasy.

Lauren picked her way inside, trying not to step on the cat while she negotiated around a pile of newspapers, a pair of old bicycles and a set of golf clubs. She could barely make out the cat's dishes from the night before, sitting on the floor. She set the fresh food and water down and picked up the dirty plates, giving Noodles's now invisible form a final pat before she straightened up and turned to go.

It was then that she noticed the smell. Along with the musty odor of damp cardboard and the sharp ammonia of the litter box, she smelled something sweet and cloying.

Noodles gave a screech, and Lauren felt something hit her on the shoulder. She screamed and dropped the dishes, and phantom hands grabbed at her in the darkness. She tried to move into a karate fighting stance, but she was penned between the mattresses and the bikes.

She couldn't see anyone, but gloved hands had locked onto her upper arms. "Let go of me," Lauren yelled in desperation. She managed to free her right arm, then delivered a swift karate chop to what she hoped was her assailant's throat. There was a gagging sound and the other hand released her. She scooted backward, lost her balance, fell on hands and knees, then scrabbled backward on all fours until she was out the garage door. A split second later, a short, dark form shot past her and took a sharp right around the side of the house.

Lauren rolled onto her side for a moment, an incredible pain shooting through her right knee where she'd fallen on it. With her free hand she carefully pushed up the leg of her sweatpants, then gingerly placed her palm over the kneecap. Fluid bubbled under her palm, but it didn't seem to be broken. Damn it! Why didn't the stupid Youngs keep their garage locked, anyway?

An older couple who lived in the unit across from Lauren's came out their back gate and hurried toward her.

"Are you all right?" the woman called.

"Yes, I'm fine," Lauren said, breathing hard.

"What happened?" the husband asked. "Are you hurt?"

"Just my knee. It'll be okay." The two of them got on either side of her and helped her stand up on her left leg.

When she'd caught her breath, Lauren explained, "Someone was in the garage. Probably a homeless person looking for a place to spend the night. I don't think they took anything."

"Those vagrants!" the woman gasped. "Did he attack you?"

"I'm not sure if he did it on purpose," Lauren said, massaging her leg. "I think maybe he was just trying to get out and ran into me in the dark. I don't think he'll be back."

"Did you get a good look at him?" the husband asked.

Lauren shook her head. "No, it was too dark, and I think he had a ski mask on."

The wife visibly shuddered. "I'll call the police."

Chapter Five

At eight o'clock on Monday morning, Bill Donelan met Julie Cox as he was unlocking his office door and she was just emerging from hers, empty coffeepot in hand.

"I swear, women have an instinct for these things," Bill said, the corners of his lips twitching. He held out a white paper sack. "Like a doughnut?"

Julie's lips pursed. "You really are a tease, Bill." But her hand reached into the bag.

"You can take one for your boss, too."

"Oh, she's not coming in this morning."

"Not coming in?" Bill's brows bunched. What was she doing? Taking another day off to hide at home while she secretly mourned for her lost friend, Andersen?

"She had a spot of trouble last night," Julie said. "Apparently a homeless person was sleeping in the garage next door. When Lauren went in to feed the cat, the tramp ambushed her and ran off. Messed up her knee pretty bad."

"Will she be okay?"

"Yes. She says it's just sprained. She'll probably be back tomorrow."

"Well, I hope she's feeling better."

Julie gave him a mischievous grin. "I'll be sure to tell her you said so."

Bill entered his office, his mind going over the altercation with Lauren that Julie had doubtless been recalling when she gave him that knowing look. He'd let off considerable steam since his argument with Lauren last Tuesday. But though he was no longer angry at her, there was still one question that was bugging him.

It was the same question that had slammed into his head when he first saw Lauren making eyes at Andersen in the Vineyard Restaurant. What in the hell had she been playing at? She obviously hadn't told him everything when she briefed him on the assignment— at least not that she'd begun an affair with Andersen. Perhaps it had been going on for some time before that day he first saw Nat leave her office.

She hadn't denied that she'd kissed the man outside her condo, only that she'd done anything wrong. But surely she didn't consider making out with a married client ethical. When he asked her if she knew Andersen was still living with Sabrina, she'd said yes; but had she been telling the truth? Had Andersen given her some line about leaving his wife, taking advantage of Lauren with the lure of his fortune and a false promise of marriage? The picture of Lauren in Nat's arms brought a sour taste to his mouth. Somehow it was hard for him to imagine Lauren being the one responsible for the tawdry affair. The thought that Andersen had used the woman and lied to her made Bill almost glad the man had met with a nasty fate.

Still brooding, Bill made himself a cup of coffee, then rolled up his sleeves and spread out the morning paper on his desk. Hands on either side, he bent over to read the headline. From there, his eyes flicked down the page, to be stopped by an all-too-familiar name. Andersen.

Mark Andersen, brother of Nathaniel Andersen, had issued a press release saying there was nothing to the rumors that his brother's death was anything but a tragic accident. The Sonoma County Sheriff's Department had declined to comment.

Bill chewed his lip as he read the article again. It was a lucky thing he'd run into Julie just now or he might not have learned Lauren was attacked. He grabbed up the paper and his keys in one hand, his jacket in the other.

As he drove, he told himself he could be all wet. Perhaps he was just using this as an excuse to make up with Lauren. She might be in no danger at all and would most probably resent his flying to her rescue like a white knight. But the fact of the matter was she was all by herself, a kid trying to run her own private investigation firm with no one to take care of her if she got in over her head. A woman foolish enough, or perhaps just vulnerable enough, to get mixed up with a disreputable cheat.

She might be too proud to accept his help, but by God, she was going to have to!

LAUREN'S DOORBELL rang just as she was finishing putting her chestnut hair back in its usual French twist. She wondered if it might be the police again. Perhaps they'd sent an officer to follow up on the report she'd made last night.

Whoever was at the door certainly didn't like waiting! The bell had been pressed three times before she limped to the foyer and looked out the peephole. It was Bill Donelan's broad frame that filled the fish-eye viewfinder.

Her heart skipped a beat and she blinked. The last person she'd expected to see was Bill! She felt a stab of pleasure, and a smile curled her lips.

But she was still in her pink terry-cloth robe with nothing on underneath! Now Bill knocked. Loudly. Damn! She'd just have to see what he wanted, then run and get dressed. She unlocked the dead bolt.

"Good morning," she said, hiding her body as she peered out at him. "There's no need to bring the door down."

Bill's shoulders visibly relaxed. "Sorry if I startled you, but Julie told me you were attacked in the neighbor's garage last night."

Was that what he was so upset about?

"Yes, but it was really nothing." Robe or no, she couldn't leave him standing out there. She tightened the sash at her waist before stepping back. "Come in, please. I told Julie I was staying home, then the knee felt a little better, so I was just getting ready to go in."

Bill picked her newspaper off the stoop and stepped inside. Lauren started to tell him to help himself to some coffee while she dressed, but he spoke first.

"Did you report the incident to the police?"

"Yes, though I debated about it first." She fingered the rolled pink collar as she looked up into his intent brown eyes. "I feel sorry for anyone who's forced to take refuge in a drafty garage. These nights have been brutal. But I was worried that it could happen again and it might be some child putting his bike away who'd be hurt next."

Bill nodded. "I think you did the right thing, but you can stop pretending it was just a vagrant. Let's go in here. I'd like to ask you a few questions."

Before she could object, he caught her elbow and walked her into the living room. His touch was as gentle yet powerful as she remembered, supporting her bad side as he shortened his pace to match her somewhat halting gait.

He helped her ease into a chair at the table in the open dining area but remained standing himself.

"Now, tell me, did you get a good look at the attacker?"

Lauren started to cross her legs, then remembered her nakedness. She held his eyes while one hand pulled the robe tightly together across her knees. "No. The person was wearing a ski mask, and the garage light was off, so it was pretty dark."

"How long have you been feeding the neighbors' cat? They were away on vacation?"

"Yes, I always do it for them. They've been gone a little over a week."

"Was the light broken?"

She sighed. He'd probably scold her, but she didn't have time to think of a fib. "No, it's just that it's hard to reach the switch, so I don't usually bother."

"Usually or ever?"

Lauren frowned. What was he getting at? "Ever."

"All right. Did you get a feeling for the man's height?"

"Short, I think. Maybe five-four or -five."

He placed one palm on the table and leaned toward her. Looking down, Lauren noticed how his huge chronometer watch looked perfectly in scale on his thick wrist, and the back of his hand was dusted with curling dark hairs that blended with his olive skin. "Build?" he said.

She swallowed and looked up. "Slender I'd say, but strong."

"What kind of ski mask?"

She wasn't used to being interrogated like this, and she knew she had every right to tell him so. A snappy retort offered itself: *Why don't you read the police report?* But she found she had no desire to use it. "It was one of those knitted masks that fits over the entire head," she answered, "and dark clothing. I've no idea what the eye or hair color was."

Bill straightened, and the scar on his cheek rippled as he ran his tongue over the inside of his jaw. He remained thoughtful for a moment, then seemed satisfied.

"Why don't you get a cup of coffee and tell me why the third degree," Lauren said, curiosity making her forget her state of undress. She'd never seen a man so purposely intent.

"Thanks." He walked around the breakfast counter to the coffeemaker and Lauren told him where to find the mugs. When he returned, he set the cup down and drew the rubber band from her morning paper. "I came over to show you this," he said, pointing to the front page.

Bill took the seat next to her as he waited for her to read the story. When she looked up at him, aqua eyes wide, he said, "The sheriff is being pretty tight-lipped about it, but it's ten to one they suspect foul play since they haven't corroborated the brother's statement."

"They think it's murder," Lauren said, eyes distant.

"Quite possibly."

"And you think the attack on me is connected with Nat?"

"It seemed rather too coincidental, so I decided to ask you."

Lauren's eyes flashed as they met his. "I have an idea who did this. The person who jumped me in the garage was wearing a French perfume I recognized. It's very expensive."

Bill's brows shot up. "The attacker was a woman?"

"I'm certain of it."

"Why didn't you tell me it was a woman?"

Lauren looked smug. "You didn't ask me about sex." Realizing too late the double entendre, her cheeks reddened.

"That doesn't mean I wasn't interested," he answered in kind, his lips puckered as he held back a laugh.

Lauren squeezed the robe's lapels together at her neck. "Anyway—" she pronounced the word with starched dignity "—we both know a woman with a motive for killing Nat Andersen."

"Mrs. Andersen." Bill hated to say it and wished it wasn't so. Lauren had proved herself a thoughtful, if impulsive, woman. He didn't want her blaming herself for Sabrina bumping her husband off in a jealous rage.

Lauren shifted in her seat, but she looked more grim than guilty. "When she appeared in the restaurant, she seemed resigned to the divorce. But she also said Nat and I would regret it." She suppressed a shiver, then became lost her in her own thoughts. "Tampering with a car is such a cliché way to kill someone," she murmured doubtfully.

"But one hundred percent effective in this case."

"You're right about that." Lauren's hands balled into fists in her lap. "I hate to think that someone murdered Nat and they're going to get away with it."

Watching her face, he couldn't tell whether her anger was motivated by a sense of justice or feelings of revenge for a lost lover. The first thought filled him with admiration, the second, with jealousy.

"I wonder who the sheriff suspects?" Lauren mused.

Though they both knew she might be in danger, it was clear to Bill she wasn't afraid. A gleam he'd never seen before was beginning to light her eyes. He was determined to find out if she was being targeted and to make sure she stayed out of harm's way. But at the same time he found her keenness to pursue the villain mildly arousing.

"We could ask what they've got on the case," he suggested. "I know a few faces at the sheriff's office, but not very well. However—" he gave her an appraising look "—I wouldn't be surprised if *you* have a contact there."

Lauren couldn't help grinning a little proudly. "You're right, I do." Her eyes returned to the newspaper. "And I wouldn't mind asking him what's happening on this case."

"Mind if I come along?"

Lauren sighed. The man was no shrinking violet. He was planted like Gibraltar in her living room, and it was clear he wouldn't be put off by some vague answer, such as she'd think about it and get back to him later. She had to decide here and now if she wanted him in on this. If it turned out to be murder, she wanted to help nail the killer, and there would be more work than she could handle by herself. Bill had proved he was up to the mark with that excellent report he'd turned in, but could she trust him with her sources?

A private investigator's confidential sources were her most important business asset. It had taken her

father years to gain the complete trust of her contact
at the sheriff's office, and she couldn't afford to lose
him to another P.I. Lauren's eyes narrowed as she
considered Bill's rugged, expectant face. Was he just
looking for work, or did he want to steal her contacts?

To give herself time to think, she got up and walked
into the kitchen to pour herself a coffee. She could
hear the clock's loud ticking in the silence that had
fallen. It reminded her forcefully that she'd been alone
the past three days. The thought of walking into the
sheriff's department by herself was suddenly so depressing she wanted to curse.

The truth was she was sick to death of working
alone. She missed terribly the old days when she'd
worked cases with her father or one of the other investigators.

She sipped her coffee as she leaned against the
kitchen counter and berated herself. Thoughts like
these should have no relevance to her decision. She
should be weighing the potential threat Donelan
posed. But was that really so much? He was the new
kid on the block, a P.I. with no reputation. It would
be years before his agency posed any kind of threat to
hers, if it survived at all, so why shouldn't she let him
tag along?

"Okay, why not?" she responded, taking her fate
in her hands. "We can go right there as soon as I
dress."

Bill nodded. "I'll wait for you, then take my car and
meet you at the sheriff's office."

A sudden certainty that she'd done the right thing rose in her heart and spread relief through her chest. She smiled to herself. Donelan really was something! The way he'd barged in here, taking charge and making her safety his business. He sat there at her table, bigger than life, totally assured, his giant, well-muscled body making the dining set look child-size. It was almost as if, from the moment he'd read that newspaper story, she'd had no choice at all.

Bill waited for Lauren to go change, but for some reason she remained standing on the other side of the breakfast counter, her cup cradled in her elegant hands. Jewellike eyes studied him from the perfect oval of her face. Then little lines appeared at the corners as her expression turned whimsical.

"I've just been wondering," she said, obviously giving in to some nagging impulse, "do you, ah, have any hobbies?"

The question wasn't what he'd expected, but he answered, "Sure. Old movies. I've got a library of videotaped classics and a small book collection on the subject. I play golf occasionally. I'm a Big Brother," he hurried on, "and whenever I can get a chance, I head up to the mountains for some camping and fishing."

Lauren smiled to herself—she'd known it! "Do you hunt, too?" she asked.

"I used to. I might take it up again now that I've moved back north," he said, unconsciously running his index finger over the scar on his cheek.

Lauren noticed the gesture. "Is that how you got the scar? A hunting accident?"

"Yes, as a matter of fact, on a deer-hunting trip."

She hesitated, curiosity probably warring with her good manners, then gave in, as he'd thought she would. "I hope you don't mind me asking, but, ah, how did it happen?"

Bill leaned back and propped his ankle on his other knee. "A buddy and I were out early one morning when we accidentally disturbed a rogue bear. It was a big male. Usually animals will give you a wide berth, but this bugger came out of nowhere and charged my friend. I shouted to distract it, then fired as it literally came down on top of me."

Lauren shuddered, her eyes wide. "Did it claw you badly?"

"No, luckily my first shot caught it right through the heart. I wouldn't have had time for a second. I came close to losing a few parts...."

Lauren's eyes flicked involuntairly below Bill's belt.

"...like my head," he finished with a grin. "But I was lucky."

"Well." Lauren hid her flaming cheeks by turning and shoving her cup into the sink. "I'd better get ready, I won't be a minute."

She hurried to her bedroom, then glanced out the window at the sky before slipping out of her robe. The weekend had been miserable and cold, but this morning's fog was burning off early, promising a mild, sunny day.

She slid open her closet door and automatically reached for her gray pin-striped suit, then paused, feeling an impulse to wear something more feminine for a change. She had several outfits for work—a wool pantsuit, two suits with midcalf skirts, several pairs of wool slacks and half a dozen oxford-cloth shirts—all of them in somber colors and usually worn with flats.

Lauren bit her lip. They'd be meeting with Ed Ramsey soon, so she couldn't go completely native. She pulled out her powder-blue wool-crepe suit, the one that picked up the color of her eyes. It had a straight skirt and a bolero jacket with capped sleeves. She donned a cream-colored silk shell and the skirt, then eased on her taupe heels and tried walking in them. Her knee gave her no problem. Standing at the dresser, she added a short pearl necklace and studs. Very nice.

Her eyes fell on the gold-capped perfume atomizer and she hesitated. She didn't often use it, since P.I.'s usually needed to blend in with their surroundings, not stand out. But what the heck—it was just one day. She gave her throat a liberal spray.

As she entered the living room, jacket slung over one shoulder, Bill looked up from the sports section of the newspaper.

"That was quick," he commented, then stopped, arrested by the sight of her. Knowing she'd fallen, he detected the slight puffiness and discoloration of her right knee beneath the sheer hose, but the other leg was as perfect and shapely as a Grecian vase. She bent over to pick up her purse, and Bill was mesmerized. Her bottom—so clearly defined beneath the stretched fabric of her skirt—was a regular work of art!

He gave a low, admiring whistle. "Lady, you're likely to catch more than criminals in that outfit."

Lauren shrugged as she straightened and provocatively lowered her lashes, even as caution and common sense screamed at her.

"My contact's a leg man," she said. Well, she told herself, flirtatious as it sounded, it was the truth!

LAUREN WAS a skilled driver who'd developed eyes in the back of her head from years of doing surveillances. But Bill Donelan was even more skilled, and he was waiting for her outside the Sonoma County Hall of Justice when she arrived.

She had tried to keep him in sight as they drove, but he'd lost her before she reached the freeway.

"How did you get here? Fly?" she teased as she joined him.

The corners of his mouth tweaked up. He liked this new side to the lady P.I. "No, ma'am. I swear I didn't break the law. The lights were simply in my favor."

"Well, if I'm ever chased by an angry subject, I'm going to think of you and wish you were at the wheel."

I just might be, Bill told himself.

They passed through a breezeway into the building's courtyard. A few people lounged on the concrete seats by the reflecting pool, others hurried in and out of the county clerk's office or headed for the stairway leading to the municipal courtrooms on the second floor.

Side by side, the two detectives crossed the courtyard and entered double doors beneath large white letters that read Sheriff. Several people were ahead of them, waiting for the attention of two women in street clothes who manned the information desk. When it was her turn, Lauren stepped forward, handed the clerk her business card and asked if Captain Ed Ramsey could spare her a few minutes. The clerk made a call, and moments later a paunchy man of about sixty in a khaki uniform walked up behind the counter and waved to her.

"Hi, Lauren. Great to see you. Come on in." He held open the gate so she could pass through. Bill followed her, and she prayed one last time she wasn't making a mistake by bringing him here. If Ramsey told them something in confidence and Bill let it get around, the captain would probably never speak candidly with her again.

"This is my associate, Bill Donelan . . . Captain Ed Ramsey," she said as the two men shook hands.

Ramsey led them through a warren of putty-colored metal desks to his office in the back and asked his secretary to bring them some coffee, then closed the door behind them.

"So what brings you here?" he asked as they took seats. "I haven't seen you since, ah . . ."

"My father's funeral?" Lauren said, clear-eyed. She smiled. "I didn't realize it had been that long."

Ramsey relaxed. "How's the agency doing?"

"Fine," Lauren fudged, "though I wouldn't mind if a century passes before we see another recession."

"Me, too," Ramsey said. "It's about time the American people had a break. Crime rate's up, too, and I think the economy's to thank for it. But I don't think you're here to discuss economics."

"No, actually, I'd like to know what you can tell me about the Nathaniel Andersen case. Preferably everything!" She wrinkled her nose and laughed. It was a sound like chiming bells, and Ramsey looked enchanted.

Bill silently chalked up another one for Lauren. She was always so truthful and serious he hadn't realized she was also skilled in the P.I.'s essential art of manipulating a subject.

"I'm glad you're not asking much," Ramsey said with a grin. They all chuckled, then Ramsey leaned forward and his face grew serious. "I have to ask you first what your interest is in this case."

Lauren, too, got down to business. "Nat Andersen was a client of mine. He was a nice guy, and I assume, from reading this morning's paper, that you're fairly sure it wasn't an accident." She gave the captain an old-boy's-network smirk.

Ramsey nodded. "Yes, and the kids *are* having a little trouble getting going on this one, so I'll tell you about it—*if* you're prepared to do some real work and help us scare up some leads."

"I'd love to." Lauren crossed her legs, momentarily diverting Bill's attention.

Ramsey, too, leaned forward on his desk, his eyes covertly straying over her limbs before he cleared his throat and continued, "By the way, I've got Schroeder and Bernet on this, and they're both kind of pouter pigeons, so whatever you do, don't let them know you've talked to me. They'd go through the roof." He shook his head in disgust as he picked up the phone receiver, then asked his secretary to bring in the Andersen case files. A few minutes later, the young woman appeared with their coffee and two thick manila folders.

The captain explained, "I can't give you copies of the reports, naturally, but I'll summarize it all for you. If you've got a memory as good as your old man's, I know you won't have any trouble remembering it."

Ramsey opened the top folder and pressed back several sheets before beginning. "Andersen lives on Hood Mountain, has a large private home, sort of a mini-estate, that he had built there. Last Wednesday night, the Italian chauffeur, Dirk DiMucci, drove him home in his limousine from the office. They arrived at the house about five-thirty and parked the car in the detached garage. Andersen went inside and was served dinner in the dining room by the housekeeper at six. At about the same time, the chauffeur left to spend the evening with his sister's family in Santa Rosa—it was his regular night off.

"At approximately seven-forty the Andersen's butler, Thomas Hinshaw, answered his employer's phone. It was a woman asking to speak to Mr. Andersen."

"I thought the butler was in a coma," Bill said.

"He was until yesterday morning. He won't be able to see visitors for a few days, but he came to long enough to give a statement. When Hinshaw asked who the caller was, she said she was a security guard at the Micom plant and told him the place had been broken into. Andersen took the call in his study, where he'd retired to work after finishing supper."

"I take it the call was bogus?" Lauren said.

"Yes. There's only one woman on the security force at the plant, and she wasn't on duty that night. However, Andersen's number is posted in the security office, so even though it's unlisted, it would have been easy for someone to get it.

"Five minutes after Andersen took the call, he telephoned Dirk DiMucci at the sister's home, and told DiMucci to meet him at Los Alamos Road and Highway 12 so he could drive him to the plant. Andersen emerged from the study and asked the butler to drive with him to the bottom of the hill so he could bring DiMucci's car back after the rendezvous.

"Andersen took the wheel of the Mercedes limousine. Shortly after leaving the level grounds of the estate and heading down the mountain, the brakes began to fail. Hinshaw reports that Andersen was cursing and pumping the brakes, but they'd gone to mush."

"You have evidence the brakes were tampered with?" Bill asked.

"Unfortunately, no. When the car went over the embankment and hit the rocks, its gas tank exploded on impact. As you know, it's been cold but there's been no rain since Thanksgiving, and the dried grass made the fire extremely hot—burned up the tires, hoses, belts, everything but the metal framework. We found a set of skid marks at the edge of the cliff, probably from the front tires, but that would be consistent with Andersen swerving to avoid a deer or a falling rock, or just plain missing the curve in the dark and then jamming on the brakes when he realized he was going over. We couldn't find any trail of spilled brake fluid on the road. In fact, if it wasn't for the butler's testimony, we would never have suspected a mechanical failure."

"There was no sign of brake fluid leaking onto the floor of the garage?" Bill asked.

"We checked the garage but there wasn't any fluid where the car was parked. That's what makes it so suspicious. Besides, Andersen bought the car used just a couple of weeks ago. According to the chauffeur it was an upgrade from the Lincoln limo he had before, smaller but easier to maneuver on the mountain, more luxurious inside, bulletproof glass and so forth. Andersen got it through a wholesaler, and I think the maintenance records just came in...." Ramsey flipped through the pages with a frustrated air and finally found what he wanted. "It was owned by a party in Palo Alto who regularly maintained it. It only had fifteen thousand miles on it and was serviced at a reputable Mercedes dealership right before Andersen bought it. So there shouldn't have been anything wrong with those brakes."

Lauren and Bill exchanged a we-were-right look. "What would someone have had to do to make the brakes fail like that?" Lauren asked.

Bill said, "The Mercedes is a rear-wheel drive, so the tamperer probably went for the rear brakes. It would be easy enough to slide under the car and loosen the feed line to the rear brakes' metering valve. Disabling the brakes from underneath would also avoid setting off the limo's car alarm."

Lauren was having some trouble picturing the procedure, but Ramsey nodded. "That's how we figure they probably did it. The nut must have been backed off to the last couple of threads, but the fire caused the brass metering valve to melt over the nut, so we have no proof it was loosened. But if it was, there would only be a few spurts of brake fluid going over the differential housing the first couple of times Andersen applied the brakes, nothing more, which would explain why we didn't find any fluid on the road. Normally the front brakes by themselves would be enough to hold the car, which they did on the flat drive leading off the estate, but once Andersen started down the mountain, he wouldn't have had a chance."

"Who had access to the garage that evening?" Lauren asked.

"DiMucci has an apartment above the garage with both inside and outside steps that give access to it. The side door to the garage and the stairs to the apartment are both away from the house, so someone could have sneaked in. There's no sign of forced entry, but DiMucci isn't sure if he locked the outer door when he went out that night. The big doors the cars pass through can only be operated from switches inside the house and the garage.

"No one in the house noticed anything unusual that night, but the housekeeper was busy in the kitchen and dining room, both of which are at the back of the house. After she served Andersen dinner and cleaned up, she went down to her room in the basement to watch television. The butler was in his office all evening going over the household accounts, and Andersen's study doesn't face the front, either, so someone could easily have jumped the wall around the property and gotten into the garage unobserved. The only one in a room that evening that faced the garage was Andersen's wife, Sabrina. Her bedroom is on the second floor, but she'd eaten dinner alone before Andersen got home, went straight up to bed, took a sleeping pill and dropped off. She didn't hear or see anything."

Lauren said, "If someone wanted to make sure the brakes would go out on the way down the mountain, where the car couldn't slow down and was sure to crash, they'd have to have rigged it just before Nat was called to the plant."

"Exactly," Ramsey agreed. "Fixing the brakes that way isn't a difficult job if you have the know-how and the proper tool. There was a ten-millimeter flare wrench among the tools on a workbench in the garage. We checked it for prints but only found Di-Mucci's.

"Our biggest problem has been establishing a motive. In his will, Andersen left the house, his personal property and a modest annuity to his wife—it's more of a token than anything, but he wasn't necessarily slighting her because she's rich in her own right, being the heir to the Falletti Winery. His biggest asset, his ownership of Micom, Inc., he divided between his two brothers. However, each of the brothers already runs his own company—gifts from their father. Mark Andersen runs a major logging operation outside of Seattle, and Peter Andersen has a small-tool-manufacturing concern in Michigan. Both brothers are very successful, so there's no money motive, and there's no evidence of brotherly or marital squabbles." Ramsey paused to take a sip of his coffee before continuing. "The younger brother, Mark, has been on a visit here since before the accident—he's been staying on the estate. But the day of the crash he was out with old friends wine-tasting in the Napa Valley and didn't return to the house until ten-thirty when he learned of his brother's death.

"However, though we can't find anyone with a motive, the crank phone call and the brakes going out so suddenly seem like too much of a coincidence to not be connected."

"Whoever planned this did a good job," Lauren mused, her face set in concentration. "About the only thing the killer didn't foresee was the fact that Nat would take the butler with him and end up with a witness."

"Whoever called may not have anticipated Hinshaw's answering the phone, either," Bill added.

"It was a private line," Ramsey agreed. "The staff didn't usually answer it, but Andersen was indisposed when the call came in." Ramsey clapped his hands down on the desk. "I've got a meeting to go to in a few minutes, but I can see you two aren't going to let the grass grow under your feet! I'm glad you decided to take an interest in this case, Lauren. And I may be able to give you a little added incentive." He leaned forward, and Lauren looked at him curiously.

"There's a spot coming vacant in the District Attorney's Office for an outside, independent investigator—that is, if you could handle the additional work."

Lauren's heart skipped a beat and a hungry look leapt to her eyes. "No problem," she said.

"The D.A. is an old buddy of mine. We golf together up at Fountaingrove." Ramsey paused meaningfully. "Any P.I. who can bring me evidence that will lead to the arrest and conviction of Andersen's killer will certainly have my recommendation for the post."

Lauren blinked; she didn't dare start breathing again. This was just the opportunity she needed! She'd do anything to get a client like the district attorney.

"That would be great, Captain," Lauren said, trying to let her enthusiasm show without sounding giddy. "I would very much like to be considered for the job. We'll get right on the case and I'll get back to you in a day or two to let you know our progress."

"Before we go," Bill said, glancing at Lauren, "we should get the phone numbers for the Andersen estate." He looked expectantly at the captain. "There must be several lines going into a household that size."

Ramsey hesitated only a moment before flipping through the report. "There's the line Andersen took the call on and a private number for Mrs. Andersen...separate numbers for the housekeeper...and yes, DiMucci's apartment. The butler probably has his own phone for his bedroom in the basement, but he's still in the hospital, so they didn't bother to get it. I'll give you the other numbers." He scribbled on a slip of paper and handed it to Bill as he rose.

"I wish you luck." Ramsey said as he showed the pair out. He looked at Lauren from under lowered brows. "And don't forget what I said about the D.A."

There was no scamming in Lauren's voice as she said, "Believe me, Captain, I won't."

Chapter Six

It was midafternoon as the two sleuths headed for Hood Mountain and the Andersen estate with Bill at the wheel of his Ford. After leaving the sheriff's office, they had formed a plan. Bill would interview Sabrina at her home, posing as an investigator for a fictitious life insurance company. Bill had phoned the estate and made an appointment with Sabrina for three-thirty.

Bill felt good as he piloted the car out of town. He and Lauren had fallen into an easy partnership, the quickness of which both surprised and pleased him. He was rapidly gaining new respect for her skills as a detective, and Lauren, too, seemed to have realized her earlier error in labeling him a rookie. She'd been grateful and unhesitant when he offered to covertly interview Sabrina, a task she obviously couldn't do herself. The issues that had divided them in the past week seemed to have become moot, and he was happy to let them pass.

"I'm surprised you haven't mentioned Chuck Caine as a suspect," he remarked as they sped past a small shopping center on the outskirts of Santa Rosa. "You said Caine threatened Andersen down in Pebble Beach."

Lauren smoothed out her powder-blue skirt and gave Bill a sidelong glance. "Actually I did think of him—last Friday when I first learned of Nat's death. That same morning I spotted a piece in the business section about a speech Caine gave at a special meeting of the Bohemian Club in San Francisco the night of the accident. I called a friend who attended the meeting. He told me Caine arrived in San Francisco for cocktails at six and didn't leave the meeting until ten. It's an hour's drive from Santa Rosa to the city, so Caine couldn't have been on the Andersen property between six and eight when the limousine was tampered with."

Bill nodded. "Good work. I didn't realize you'd suspected foul play before I burst in on you this morning."

Lauren smiled at the memory. "I didn't. It was just a passing thought, and I discarded it after I checked out Caine's alibi."

Bill turned left onto the road leading up Hood Mountain. From the corner of her eye, she saw him reach beneath his jacket to his shirt pocket and draw out a pack of cigarettes and a flat, stainless-steel lighter. He glanced over at her, as if waiting for her to object. She met his eyes without censure, then looked away. She didn't smoke, but if Bill did, she wasn't going to give him a hard time about it. Lord knew there were enough people, like her mother, who made others miserable with their criticisms.

"It's ironic," Bill said conversationally. "All the time I lived in L.A. with the smog, I kept telling myself I should cut back, smoke less. Then I moved up here where the air is clear, and I hardly smoke at all anymore."

The corners of Lauren's mouth tilted up and she nodded.

They were gaining altitude quickly, passing through an area covered with oak, brush and lichen-covered boulders. There were only a few homes up here—some in clearings next to the road, others accessible down dirt roads that led into the trees.

Bill seemed content to watch the scenery, but Lauren felt happy and talkative. "So now that you've cut down, do you plan to quit? Smoking, I mean."

"Oh, no." He shook his head emphatically. "Life's no fun without *some* vices."

Lauren's brow wrinkled. "But isn't it harder to keep yourself to just a cigarette or two a day than it is to quit completely?"

Bill tamped the cigarette out in the ashtray. "No, not for me. Not when you know what you want."

Lauren was curious; he sounded so nonchalant, so sure of himself. "Do you always know what you want?"

"Yes, I think I know what I want," he answered deliberately, his eyes shifting from the roadway to rake her from head to waist. Emboldened, Lauren returned the once-over.

Bill's face split in a grin as he focused again on the road. After a moment he said, "I'm waiting."

Lauren was lost. "Waiting for what?"

"For you to ask me what it is I want."

Lauren's heart beat faster, as though she was stepping onto a fast carnival ride. She covered her mouth with her hand to suppress a girlish giggle. "I know I'll probably regret this, but go ahead."

"Three things," he began, his tone turning serious in a manner she hadn't expected. "I want my business to get off the ground and start showing a profit within two years. And I want to earn a reputation as the best private eye in Santa Rosa. And..."

Lauren held her breath, her pulse pounding in her ears.

"...I want to take a look at that patch of road up ahead."

"What?"

He pointed through the windshield.

A feeling of disappointment dampened her. Why in the world had she wanted him to say one of his dreams was to make love to her? Pray God he hadn't read her mind! Or probably he had, and had used it as an opportunity to tease her.

She forced her cheeks not to flush as she followed the direction he indicated. There was an area of charred hillside several hundred yards ahead.

"I see what you mean," she said. "That must be where the limousine went over."

Bill drove around the bend and brought the car to a stop on the shoulder. With a small frown he said, "Let's take a look."

Together they climbed out of the Taurus and walked up the road. The rocks and gravel along the pitted asphalt were sooty from where the fire had crept up the hill and singed them. Down the blackened slope, they could see an outcropping of granite the size of a large toolshed and the remains of a small clump of oak trees that had grown next to it. There were drag marks where a crane had lifted the demolished car to the roadside.

"Lucky there was a natural firebreak there," Bill said, motioning to where the slope turned from grass to a rocky hillside farther up the road.

"Mmm," Lauren murmured in agreement. She began walking up the road, and though the afternoon was warm, her arms were folded tightly across her chest. Bill followed.

Lauren noted a place on the up-slope side of the road where the rock above the shoulder was abraded. "The limousine must have bounced into the hill here, ricocheted off and gone over."

Bill just nodded. They stood gazing mutely about for another minute, then Bill said, "Come on, let's get going."

When they pulled up to the white, wrought-iron gates of the Andersen estate, Bill used the phone to announce himself. Past the gate, they wound along the wooded hillside, then emerged in a clearing where the mountain slope had been leveled out to accommodate a large house. Lauren ducked down out of sight.

Bill took in the two-story manse, painted a pale, creamy yellow with tan trim. A hedge-lined circular drive took him past the house. Between the house and separate garage there was a gap where the trees had been felled to provide a panoramic view of Santa Rosa in the valley below.

He parked on a concrete pad just beyond the garage and cut the engine. Since entering the grounds he hadn't seen a soul. He put his arm around the back of Lauren's seat. "No one's around, if you want to take a look."

She bobbed up and carefully studied the buildings through the passenger-door window. "I've got an idea! With the view they've got, there must be some kind of deck off the back of the house. Why don't you have Sabrina go out there for your interview with her. Tell her you've got asthma or something and need the fresh air. I'll sneak around the back and hide beneath the deck so I can listen in."

"Whatever you say, but be careful and don't let any of the servants catch you."

"Yes, Dad," Lauren said in a little girl's voice. She turned to him with a teasing smile and realized he'd been staring at her profile. His arm rested just behind her shoulders. Perhaps it was only the dim interior of the car, but his pupils appeared dilated and luminous.

"Believe me, honey, I'm not your Daddy," he drawled.

Lauren's heart skipped a beat.

"But you'd better get down before someone sees you," he said, moving his free arm to cup her shoulder with his palm.

"Oh, of course." His touch was disconcerting in the extreme as she let him gently push her down onto her side on the seat.

"Comfy?" he said huskily.

"Not very, thank you." She squished around a little till she was almost on her back, and avoided his eyes.

He leaned down, his long torso stretching over her so they were almost eye to eye. He moistened his lower lip with one slow sweep of his tongue. His mouth looked firm and smooth and enticing.

"How about a kiss for good luck?" he whispered.

Caught between desire and dismay, unable to move from under him, unsure of what she was feeling, Lauren squeaked.

Bill obviously took that for a yes, because he lowered his head to hers, his nose just barely passing hers as he brushed her lips.

He meant to give her a quick peck, but as he met her mouth he found himself drawn in, wanting a taste of her. Her lips were sweet and ripe and warm.

Against her better judgment, Lauren responded, moving her mouth in tandem with his. As they caressed one another's flesh, something deep and wild and free leapt between them. For a moment she thought he might demand more, seek entrance to the cavern of her mouth with his tongue, but he hesitated. She reached up and tried to draw him closer, grasping the rough, tactile wool of his lapels.

As quickly as he'd descended on her, he pulled back. Dazed, Lauren opened her eyes to find him gazing at the front door. "Give me two minutes, then come around the back," he said, and left her.

She lay prone on the seat, her mind faintly registering a woman's voice mixed with Bill's and the front door closing. She finally raised herself up on her elbows, strangely shaken. It had only been a kiss, not even a deep one, but somehow it had felt so... intimate. As though she'd gone all the way with him here on the seat. As though...well, as though in some mystical way he'd branded her as his own.

Her hands fumbled at her hair. She felt sure it must be in a mess around her shoulders, like a wanton woman's. She pulled down the visor and checked herself in the mirror, but except for a few stray hairs and the lost look in her eyes, she appeared much as she had when she'd dressed this morning.

Had she taken leave of her senses? Why had she let him sweep her off her feet? She should have stopped him, reprimanded him, slapped him if necessary. Why had she ever encouraged him to tease her, let him think she wanted him to kiss her? And why had she grabbed him at the last moment like she'd never let him go?

She hated being frightened, but that's what she was. She still knew almost nothing about Bill Donelan. Only a few days ago she'd been convinced he was trying to steal her clients. But she'd let him take her in with his rough, overtly masculine charm, allowed him to steer her attention from the serious business at hand. She had the terrible feeling that things were careening out of control.

How long had it been since Bill had gone inside? A minute? Two? Five? She leaned back against the headrest and squeezed her eyes shut for a moment, then opened them with a groan and quietly exited the car.

The path alongside the house sloped steeply downward, and Lauren cursed the high heels she'd chosen this morning, instead of her usual sturdy flats. At least her knee was working.

She crooked her neck up. Sure enough, there was a white stucco balustrade that no doubt surrounded a terrace atop the basement level. As the concrete path abruptly ended, Lauren stepped off it onto bare dirt and crept around the end of the house where she couldn't be seen from the walk.

It was ten minutes by her watch before she heard voices, and then footsteps, above her.

"You have a magnificent view from here, Mrs. Andersen," she heard Bill say. He was close to the balustrade above her head. "Thank you for showing it to me."

There was no reply.

"I appreciate your seeing me on such short notice," Bill's voice continued. "I'll try to keep my questions as brief as possible. First of all, were you here the night of the accident?"

Lauren thought Sabrina was going to fail to respond again, then she heard a faint, "Yes."

"Did you speak to your husband before he went out?"

"No."

"Did you see him earlier that evening?"

"No, I don't think so. I wasn't feeling well, so I went up to my room right after dinner."

Lauren nodded to herself. Sabrina's voice sounded flat, disinterested, very much as it had the night she'd met her.

"Do you know why he went out?" Bill probed gently.

"The police said he got a call about a break-in at his plant."

"Had your husband seemed troubled lately? Preoccupied?"

Lauren thought she heard Sabrina sigh. "My husband and I weren't close—we really lived separate lives. That's the way we wanted it. Funny, though, now that he's gone, I miss him more than I thought I would."

Was she still addressing Bill or talking more to herself? Lauren wished she could see the woman's face.

Abruptly Sabrina changed the subject. "I don't get visitors often. I've forgotten what to do. I should offer you something, shouldn't I? But I don't know what we have. The cook would know.... What do you like? I'd have Hinshaw mix you a drink, but he's in the hospital. Did you know my butler was in the accident, too? I'm sorry, I'd offer you something, but I'm not feeling very well.... What did you say your name was? I don't get visitors much, and I'm not used to it."

Then she asked, "Were you here before? Right after the accident?"

"My name is Bill Dover," he replied, using his alias, "and this is the first time I've been here, Mrs. Andersen."

"The police think someone killed Nat. I suppose the life insurance policy you told me about is invalid if that's true, isn't it? Who gets the money?"

"You do, ma'am."

"Really? Nat never told me. I expect you'll come to your own conclusion, no matter what anyone says. It doesn't matter. I don't care about the money.... My father is Joseph Falletti. Did you know that?" A sullenness crept into her voice. "Is that all you wanted to ask me? I think I should go in now."

Lauren heard retreating footsteps and a door closing. She peeked around the corner, then crept back up the side path and around the rear of the garage.

All seemed quiet from the garage's second-story apartment, and she was almost to the car when she heard a door open behind her. There was no time to duck out of sight. With a sigh of resignation she turned to find the dark figure of Dirk DiMucci skewering her with his gaze from the stair landing.

"Whatta *you* doing here?" he demanded. He clattered down the stairs, donning a pair of European-looking sunglasses as he came. Snug jeans and a black knit shirt accentuated his wiry figure. He planted himself barely two feet from her, elbows jutting out, hands on his belt.

Lauren stood her ground as she quickly considered the alternatives and discarded them. There was really nothing for it at this point but to tell Dirk the truth.

"I'm a private investigator, Mr. DiMucci." She kept her voice firm and level so he would realize the use of his last name was out of respect, not out of fear or an attempt to be ingratiating. She pulled her P.I.'s license from her purse and showed it to him. He stared down at it for a few moments as she continued slowly, "I was working for Mr. Andersen, and now I'm working with the Sonoma County Sheriff's Department to help determine the cause of Nat's accident."

Dirk raised his head, but the glasses were so opaque she couldn't see his eyes.

"You think it was an accident?" he said.

His accent was as thick as she remembered it from that day on the golf course. From the way his mouth was drawn in a crooked line, Lauren guessed he was skeptical about his employer's death. She raised one eyebrow and answered his question with a question, "Do *you* think it was an accident?"

He folded his arms across his chest and gave a wry little smile that seemed to say they were even. She relaxed a bit. Maybe this Italian wasn't as inscrutable as he'd seemed at first.

"You live over the garage?" she asked, indicating the apartment with a nod of her head.

"*Sí*—Yes."

"I understand you were off the night of the... accident."

"Yes, I was."

"Can you tell me why Nat Andersen called you and asked you to meet him at the bottom of the mountain? Why didn't he just drive himself to the plant?"

Dirk shrugged elaborately. "I don't know. He didn't like to drive himself nowhere. He always had me on call, waiting for him," he added sourly.

"I take it he wasn't an easy man to work for." Lauren put a touch of sympathy into her voice.

DiMucci's scowl deepened and he didn't respond. She was about to rephrase her question and try again when the front door of the house opened and Bill emerged.

"Who's that?" asked the chauffeur. "Is he with you?" The muscles of his shoulders tightened, but whether he was frightened by the big man's sudden appearance or simply angry, she couldn't tell.

"Just an associate of mine," she assured him. "Another private investigator."

"He been talking to Mrs. Andersen?"

"Yes. Is that all right?"

"She doesn't know nothing. Your friend here has no reason to bother her."

Bill came and stood beside Lauren, his hand reaching for her elbow. "Is everything okay here?"

"Yes, of course," Lauren said, then introduced the pair.

Bill extended his hand, and Dirk reluctantly took it.

"Thank you for talking to me, Mr. DiMucci," Lauren said. She handed him her business card. "If you think of anything that might be useful to the police, you can call me."

DiMucci took the card, but his chin was tilted up and the glasses pointed somewhere above their heads in a posture of dismissal. He remained frozen there as Lauren and Bill walked to the car.

Lauren's mind had been on the interview, but she was now acutely aware that in seconds she'd be alone with Bill again in his car. There was no time to waste in reestablishing a proper, safe distance between them.

"Bill," she said, getting his attention, "mind if I drive?"

His brows came together inquiringly and he hesitated a moment. "Sure. Was I exceeding the speed limit?"

"Uh...no," she said, searching for an excuse but not coming up with one.

He opened the driver's-side door for her and waited as she slid in, then handed her the keys.

There was a slight but unmistakable depression in the seat where his big frame always rested, and she was miles from the foot pedals. She fought with the seat adjustment as he climbed in beside her.

When she started the engine, the automatic shoulder belt charged forward, grazing the taut nipple of her left breast before coming to rest intimately over her chest. It gave her the strangest feeling, as though the man's car were an extension of...

"Don't forget to buckle up."

"What?" she said, her voice too loud, too high.

Bill gave her a funny look. "Your seat belt."

"Oh, yes, thank you." She ignored an absurd twinge of embarrassment as she hastily fastened the belt over her lap. This was getting absolutely ridiculous, she told herself. Get a grip! After fumbling around for what seemed like an hour, she yanked the gearshift into Reverse and backed up.

Once they were out of the circular drive, Lauren talked to cover her nervousness. "Well, Dirk certainly is a sullen customer. I don't think he had much love for his boss." She began to ask Bill if he thought Dirk could have killed Nat, then decided it would be more assertive not to ask his opinion.

Bill gave it, anyway. "I don't think Dirk did it. Not unless he's pretty dumb. For a chauffeur to sabotage his own limousine would be too obvious."

"Hmm. Dirk was upset you were talking to Sabrina. Maybe he helped her do it."

A Cadillac Allanté suddenly appeared ahead of them with a fair-haired man at the wheel. The driver grimaced and craned his neck to look at Bill and Lauren as they passed.

"Was that Mark Andersen?" Bill asked.

"It must be."

"Wonder why he's hanging around. The funeral was last week. Comforting the grieving widow, perhaps?"

"Perhaps. Speaking of the grieving widow, how did your interview with Sabrina go?"

"Were you able to hear us?"

"Yes. How did she look?"

"Well, you weren't exaggerating when you said she lacks expression. Her eyes were vacant most of the time, like she didn't give a damn about anything. At first I thought she might be on drugs, but I don't know. I want to find out if her doctor is prescribing anything for her besides the sleeping pills Ramsey mentioned."

As Lauren turned out of the estate onto Los Alamos Road, she said, "It was strange how she rambled on like that, and her mood seemed to fluctuate. That's how she acted that night in the restaurant, too. I wonder if she has some serious mental problem. Perhaps Nat didn't want to tell me how bad it really was."

Bill thought for a moment. "No, I didn't get the feeling she's insane. I think she's probably just a very unhappy woman. She's rich and young with nothing to do—no children, no job, no responsibilities even to run her own household. The housekeeper seems as efficient as a marine sergeant." He tilted his head. "Frankly I feel sorry for Sabrina. I've never seen a woman let herself go like that. It took her a long time to come downstairs when I first arrived. I'll bet she was still up there in her nightgown, and she had on this old, velour, leisure-suit type of thing with food stains on the front. She hadn't combed her hair. She was really a sorry sight."

"Did she show any emotion at all? Anger, fear, remorse?"

"Not really. It was weird. She has a large collection of dolls—they're all through the house—those big, beautiful porcelain ones that some women go crazy for. I asked her about it, and she told me she collects them."

"Maybe it's because she doesn't have any children," Lauren suggested.

"No, it's not that. I don't believe she plays with the dolls or even touches them. She just looks at them. I think in a way they fascinate her. The dolls' faces reminded me of hers, totally blank, but a lot more serene."

Lauren felt a shiver tickle her spine. "Did you get a look at the house?"

"Yes. While I waited for Sabrina I did a bit of a survey. All the rooms that were occupied that night, except for Sabrina's bedroom, are at the back of the house. So someone could have easily sneaked into the garage without being seen."

"What about the staircase from the upper floor?" Lauren asked. "Is it visible from either the breakfast room or study, where Nat spent the evening?"

"Yes, from both. It's in the center of the front hallway. But if you had the door closed or were preoccupied, someone could tiptoe down the stairs and go out unnoticed."

"Hmm." Lauren's mind began to race; she spoke quickly. "Sabrina went up to her room, ostensibly to bed, before Nat arrived home that night. From her room she had a view of the garage, so she'd have been able to watch until Dirk left for his night off. Then, while Nat was eating dinner and the servants were occupied in the back rooms on the first floor, she could have slipped out, gone into the garage through the side door with a key and fixed the limousine. When she got back to her room, she used her private telephone line to call Nat, disguise her voice and tell him there was a break-in at the plant.''

"She'd have to know more than a thing or two about cars.''

"Yes, but it's surprising what people can do when they're motivated. There must be shop manuals and things like that that show how a Mercedes works. She could have either purchased one or gotten it from the library.''

Bill frowned but didn't say anything, and silence fell between them as the Taurus sped down the highway toward town. When they were almost back at the office, she spoke again.

"I'll have to hire someone to do an around-the-clock surveillance on Sabrina, and I'll personally handle the interviews with her family and friends. I'll get to her old roommates and teachers if I need to. But the one I want to start with is her psychiatrist. Nat mentioned his name once. I think it was Ferris, Dr. Timothy Ferris.''

"I'll be glad to talk to him for you,'' Bill offered.

"No, thank you. I'll handle that one myself. I want you to do a background check on Sabrina. We'll need to check her medical records, her school records, see if the police have ever picked her up wandering around town in a daze, things like that. It's almost five, so it's too late to make any calls tonight, but I'll meet you in my office tomorrow at eight and show you what to do.''

The male P.I. shifted in his seat. "I agree it would be prudent to follow up on Sabrina, but I don't think we should waste a lot of time on it if we don't turn up anything. And if the sheriff's men haven't found a reason to suspect the Andersen brothers, I think we can forget about them for the moment, too. But what about Nat Andersen himself? I think we should check him out."

"And *I* don't."

"Then maybe you should think again."

Lauren exhaled loudly. Why was he arguing with her? Ever since they'd left the Andersen estate she'd been showing him through her body language and tone of voice that she was reclaiming her authority, taking charge. As the one who was paying him, as the one with more experience, she had every right. She'd thought he'd settle down and accept it, but he was bucking her.

She tried to keep calm. "If I had the manpower and the money I would investigate everyone who had anything to do with Nat, but Sabrina seems like the most likely suspect since she has some motive—jealousy or revenge perhaps." She didn't want to tell him it was going to take the last of her savings to hire him and the surveillance crew. "Besides," she added, "if that woman in my neighbor's garage was intentionally lying in wait for me, it *had* to be Sabrina."

"Not necessarily. You said you thought it was her because of the expensive perfume. It probably was a woman all right, but she could have worn one of those fake perfumes that mimic the name brands."

Lauren thought of the faux scent she'd sprayed on that morning in her misguided attempt to attract him.

It had cost her about two dollars at Thrifty. But though Bill had a point, this wasn't the time to admit it.

"I just think you should spread out your resources more, not concentrate on Sabrina," Bill said firmly.

"And I don't agree." She should have added that if he didn't like it, he could shove it and she'd hire someone else. It was what any responsible business-woman would do. If he objected one more time, said one more thing, she would do it. She really would.

When she gathered enough courage to look at him, he was staring at her, his wide jaw clamped menacingly.

But he didn't say anything.

Thank goodness.

Chapter Seven

The next morning at nine-thirty, Lauren hung up the phone in her office and looked at her watch. Bill had been supposed to meet her at eight.

"Julie." She walked out to the reception area. "Did Bill call, by any chance, while I was on the phone?"

"No, love."

Lauren felt a strange mixture of emotions, rather as though she'd been stood up for a date. "He must have fallen in a hole somewhere." *He's so infuriating and independent, but I hope nothing has happened to him!* She bit her lip.

She'd been extremely careful the past twenty-four hours: making sure the condo doors and windows were locked at all times, checking to see that no one was following her, watching as she entered the garage to make sure Sabrina wasn't lying in wait for her. After Dirk caught her and Bill, he may well have gone straight to Sabrina and told her who the friendly insurance man was. Lauren decided if Bill hadn't arrived by the time she returned this afternoon, she'd go looking for him herself.

"I'd try calling him," she said to Julie, "but his number's unlisted. Oh, well—" she tried to sound unconcerned "—I can't wait for him any longer. If he comes in, would you please give him this. It's a list of names to call with instructions for the background check I want him to do on Sabrina Andersen."

BILL STEPPED into the office elevator. He didn't bother to look at his watch, but he knew he was very late, and that the lady P.I. would probably be as mad as a wet hen.

Well, let her. She was being absolutely myopic about this case, so someone had to follow the other lines of inquiry. And if she was going to play the dictator with him, she could sit and wait awhile.

The kiss hadn't helped relations between them, of course. He knew he'd made a tactical error there. Too bad all his mistakes couldn't be as pleasurable as that one!

He remembered how lighthearted he'd felt as he teased her on the way up the mountain. He'd been enjoying her company more than should be legal, feeling like a kid again. The kiss had been purely a spur-of-the-moment thing. He would have been less surprised if she'd stopped him; it was her response that was the revelation. Quite a delightful one. Bill grinned.

But by the time he'd finished his interview with Sabrina, Lauren had gotten uptight again. All the way back, she'd treated him like Attila the Hun.

He stepped into his office just long enough to check the recorder for messages, then he headed next door with a decidedly wicked sense of anticipation. Lauren was cute when she was in a dither.

She was just saying goodbye to Julie when Bill walked in. "Good morning, ladies."

"Where have you been?" Lauren asked, spreading her hands at her sides in a mixture of relief and annoyance.

Unable to resist, he feigned shock. "Am I late? I hadn't realized."

"Cut the corn, Bill. I want to know where you've been."

"Don't get lathered up," he said. "Believe me, I wasn't wasting my time—or yours."

"Then you won't mind telling me where you were."

He shook his head. He wasn't going to let this escalate into a fight, but he wasn't about to let her boss him around, either.

"Listen," he said, "when the time is right, I'll tell you where I was this morning. In the meantime, we can stand here and yak, or we can get some work done."

Uncertainty wavered in Lauren's eyes.

"You've got your purse, so you must be on your way out," he said. "Have you got a lead?"

"I have an appointment with Dr. Wanda Hosmer at ten." She handed him the instructions. "Here's a list of the calls I want you to make while—"

"The TV doc, from Channel 50?" he interrupted, folding the sheets and putting them in his inner jacket pocket.

"Yes. If you get started right away—"

"Why do you want to see her?"

"She did a series on mental disorders a couple of months back and she's very knowledgeable and I wish you'd stop interrupting me!" Lauren almost stamped her foot.

Bill's eyes twinkled. "Sounds interesting. I'll go with you."

"But what about—"

He waved a hand. "I can get to it later." When she glared he said, "Sorry, I didn't mean to interrupt you again. Come on. We'll take my car."

He was already through the door ahead of her. Lauren could see that stopping him would be like stepping in front of a speeding train. She rolled her eyes at Julie and trotted after him.

"So, did you hire a surveillance team?" Bill said as they left the building.

"Yes." She wouldn't tell him she'd only been able to afford one man, and only till midnight tomorrow, but she couldn't resist complaining. "I had to go as far as Marin County to find someone. You wouldn't believe what they charge."

"It was like that in L.A. Makes you wonder what we're doing up here in Santa Rosa, doesn't it?"

His remark reminded her that she didn't know exactly where and how he'd been employed down there. Earlier that morning she'd phoned her contact in the Los Angeles area, a private eye from Orange County. He'd been out of the office, but she'd left a message asking what, if anything, he knew about a dick named Bill Donelan and to call her back.

She might have asked Bill himself, but he was scanning the street and the parking garage ahead of them, and she followed suit.

"You've been keeping your head up, I trust," he said as he put his hand on her back and hurried her through the crosswalk.

His concern touched her, but it was safer to sound impatient. "Yes, of course."

They took Bill's car. He found a spot for the Taurus on Mendocino Avenue and pumped some change into the parking meter. Across the street, in front of the cinder-block-and-concrete facade of KFTY Broadcasting, was a white Channel 50 news van.

Lauren told the receptionist they were here to see Dr. Hosmer, then they settled down on the red futons in the waiting area.

Fifteen minutes later a handsome, dark-haired woman of about forty-five, dressed in a winter-white suit, burst through the lobby doors. Lauren thought the woman's expressive face and trim build made her look like a Hollywood actress. No wonder they'd chosen her for television.

"I'm sorry I'm late, Lauren," her friend apologized as Lauren rose and they shook hands. "An emergency patient." Lauren thought she detected an added sparkle in the doctor's smile as she was introduced to the handsome male P.I.

"Any messages?" Dr. Hosmer asked, turning to the receptionist, who handed her a pink slip.

"Come on back to my dressing room," she said to Lauren and Bill, motioning them forward as she read her telephone message, then crumpled it in one hand.

They skirted behind the small studio where the noon news program was shot to a door bearing a brass plate engraved with Hosmer's name.

"Thanks for coming in early," Lauren said as they stepped into the small space, which resembled an office more than a dressing room. Bill leaned against the doorjamb so Lauren could take the single chair, and Dr. Hosmer perched on the edge of her desk.

"No problem," the doctor said, spreading her hands. "I wanted to come in to work on my notes, anyway. I'm doing a series on prostate problems starting next week."

Lauren cocked an eyebrow at Hosmer. "What is it *this* week? Athlete's foot?" She knew the other woman enjoyed a little verbal repartee.

The doctor grinned. "No, they're giving me a reprieve from the one-minute reports. I'm just answering viewers' phone calls on the air and giving my wise advice this week."

"How long is your spot?" Bill asked. "Five minutes?"

"No! It's only about three—that's all they can spare on a news program—but it's the longest three minutes of my day." Hosmer slid a finger under the collar of her silk blouse and pulled on it.

Lauren laughed at her mugging. Secretly she believed that Wanda Hosmer relished her TV stardom.

It was evident from the panache and ease with which she handled the program.

"Speaking of your reports," Lauren said, "didn't you do a series a couple of months back on mental illness?"

"Yes, over the past year I've done pieces on the more common mood and mental disorders—depression, manic depression, anorexia and bulimia, schizophrenia. Boy, we got a lot of calls after the one on depression!"

Lauren exchanged a quick glance with Bill. She had wanted to conduct this interview alone, but with Bill's six-foot-six presence filling much of the room, it was hard not to include him. "I, we, need to pick your brain a little, Wanda. I know you won't be able to give us any long-range diagnosis, but what I really want is just some background information. For instance, what are the signs of a true clinical depression?"

"A major depression, the kind that needs to be treated by a therapist, is severe and prolonged. The person with major depression feels worthless, hopeless, alone, despairing." She gestured with her hands. "They lose interest in friends, hobbies, food, sex—all the things that people normally enjoy and look forward to. A depression is considered major when it continues like that for a year or more or when it causes a person to withdraw from other people and become reclusive."

"I see," Lauren said. Well, that certainly described Sabrina Andersen, but there was more to her behavior. "And what about someone who has a blank, emotionless expression and a flat, toneless way of speaking, rather as though they're in shock. When you ask them questions, they respond in monosyllables, or else they give rambling answers and find it difficult to stay on the subject.''

"Well." Hosmer rubbed her chin. "The rambling and lack of attention could be an instance of what's called 'loosening of associations' or 'cognitive slippage and derailment,' which is one of the major symptoms of schizophrenia. Schizophrenics tend to withdraw into their own world. They often have auditory delusions where they hear voices speaking to them, or hallucinations where they see things that aren't there. The visions can be quite terrifying. And because the patient is so preoccupied with them, he or she may find it hard to interact with the outside world.''

Bill cleared his throat. "Are people with schizophrenia usually institutionalized and considered insane?''

Hosmer tilted her head. "Insanity is a legal, not psychological, term. Schizophrenia is what is properly termed a psychological disorder. Often schizophrenics are institutionalized, but sometimes a devoted family member will care for them in the home.''

"What causes it? Are they born with it?" Bill asked.

"In a manner of speaking, yes, though the symptoms usually don't appear until after childhood. Many researchers think it's a genetic brain disorder. Those with schizophrenia are very likely to have a parent with the same disorder. The disorder often first shows up in a person's late teens or midtwenties."

Lauren nodded, her blue eyes attentive, urging Hosmer to go on.

"Sometimes the symptoms come on slowly and the subject gradually becomes more reclusive, his behavior more abnormal. Sometimes the onset is sudden, set off by some very emotional, traumatic situation. Sudden onset usually occurs in those patients who already led retiring lives and who were self-preoccupied or insecure."

"I see," Lauren said. "Are schizophrenics ever violent or psychotic?"

"Schizophrenics aren't usually violent," Hosmer replied. "They're more of a threat to themselves than others. However, in certain cases, they *can* become dangerous, as when an inner voice tells them to kill someone. You've heard of David Berkowitz, the Son of Sam killer? He believed that demons inside his neighbor's dogs were telling him to kill young women. He murdered six and wounded seven others. And then there was John Hinckley, the one who very nearly assassinated President Reagan. Both Berkowitz and Hinckley were schizophrenics."

Lauren grimaced. "Is it possible that a psychiatrist might make a diagnosis of major depression when the patient, a woman, is really schizophrenic?"

Hosmer's cheek muscles rippled. "Are we talking about you, here?"

Lauren guffawed. "I was afraid you were going to ask me that. No, it's not me, I promise."

"Don't believe her," Bill interjected.

"Shut up, please." Lauren laughed and waved at him.

Hosmer was grinning, too. "I'm glad, though I didn't think you looked either morose or confused. But, yes, it is possible to misdiagnose a mental disorder. Some of the symptoms of depression and schizophrenia are similar. Reclusiveness, lack of emotion or inappropriate emotional responses—laughing when you should cry for example—not caring about personal hygiene and appearance, mood swings." The doctor's brows came together in a cautionary look. "Judging what is normal and what is abnormal can be very difficult. Psychological diagnosis is an inexact science, and even the best psychologists are sometimes wrong. Especially with something like schizophrenia, which can have remission periods where the patient acts quite normally."

Lauren wondered how straight Sabrina's doctor had been with Nat. Was it possible he hadn't fully informed Nat of the extent of his wife's illness? "Are therapists required by their oath or by law not to misrepresent or hide the true nature of a patient's condition?"

"You mean is the doctor obligated to come out and say if he thinks a patient has a certain disorder? No. Quite the contrary. Often psychiatrists hesitate to make a pronouncement that someone has a mental disorder because it automatically attaches a stigma to that patient. Family and friends may shy away because of it. The only reason for attaching a label like that is to make an official diagnosis so the patient can be admitted to a mental health institution, receive money for treatment from their insurance company, and so on.''

Hosmer took a deep breath and leaned forward. ''Having said all that, I'm almost afraid to ask why you asked. You have a relative, perhaps?''

Lauren shook her head. ''The only disorder in my family is chronic workaholism.''

''Ah, yes, the disease of the eighties. It's going out of fashion now, though I admit it's personally my favorite fixation, as well.''

''We're working on a case where one of the subjects is a bit strange,'' Bill said. ''I'm sorry, but we can't say more than that.''

Hosmer gave him a big smile. ''I understand. I hope I've been helpful.''

''You have,'' Lauren assured her as she rose. ''Thanks for your time. We don't want to take you away from your work any longer.''

They walked to the studio entrance, the doctor chatting with Bill while Lauren was lost in her own thoughts. At the studio door, she realized it was time to say goodbye and make the teasing exchange that usually passed between her and Wanda. When she glanced up, she was surprised by the grave frown that had replaced the doctor's usual self-possessed expression.

''Just one thing, Lauren,'' she said, her troubled eyes meeting and holding her friend's. ''I don't want to frighten you, but if you're involved in a case where there's a violent schizophrenic, I can't warn you too strongly to be careful. It doesn't pay to underestimate someone with this condition. Their looks can deceive you. These people may appear totally out of it, but mentally they're plenty together and cunning enough to plan a murder and execute it. And unless you lock them up, you can't stop them—they're like kamikazes. You see, when you've got a persecution complex, with a voice in your head demanding day and night you kill someone, you'll do anything to satisfy that voice. Anything to silence it.''

BILL AND LAUREN didn't say much until they were almost back to the office. Bill seemed to have been sobered by the interview as much as Lauren. It was he who finally spoke. "I've got a lunch date I have to get to, but I'll be back by, say, two-thirty.''

"That's a long lunch,'' she remarked, thinking of the list of calls he seemed to be avoiding.

"I know, but it's an old friend and we haven't seen each other in some time.''

He's meeting a woman, she thought. A stab of jealousy contorted her face. Bill saw it and chuckled.

"I'd invite you along, but—''

"Never mind! I've got plans of my own, thank you.'' She straightened rigidly in her seat.

He pulled up in front of their office building and double-parked. His hand restrained her as she gathered her purse. "I know I don't have to tell you this,'' he said, "but after what Dr. Hosmer's just told us, be careful. Do you have a gun?''

"Yes. I've got one in my desk, and I cleaned it last night."

The lines in Bill's forehead disappeared. "Good girl." He patted her thigh, but took his hand back with a frown when she flinched.

LAUREN SPENT the next couple of hours lunching with Dr. Timothy Ferris's receptionist.

Once she'd driven to the building that housed Sabrina's psychiatrist, it was easy to locate an empty office suite and fabricate the story that she, Lauren, was the secretary for a doctor who was shortly to rent the vacant space. She introduced herself to Dr. Ferris's receptionist, a primly dressed young woman named Heather Miller, and offered to take her to lunch. They went to a Chinese restaurant nearby.

At first Lauren hoped the woman was just shy, but Heather proved to be genuinely reserved. She was disinclined to offer information about herself, and not curious enough about Lauren to ask questions in return. Lauren had worked successfully with such private people before, so she kept the conversation carefully neutral until Heather began to warm to her toward the end of the meal.

"Did you read in the newspapers about Nathaniel Andersen?" Lauren asked, making her move. "That man who was killed in a suspicious car crash in Santa Rosa last week?"

"Yes, I heard about it on the news," Heather said, taking the last bite of her fried rice and laying down her fork.

"I noticed the story especially," Lauren continued, "because Mrs. Andersen was a patient of my boss's a couple of years ago. Dr. Gordon is a psychiatrist, too."

Lauren hoped Heather would jump in and exclaim, "What a coincidence—Mrs. Andersen is one of *our* patients!" But all the young woman said was "Mmm."

"Yes . . ." Lauren thought quickly. "She was a patient of ours for about a year, then she left. The doctor was disappointed because her treatment wasn't completed, and I always wondered if she didn't leave us for some other psychiatrist."

"It's possible," Heather said. "Patients often do that if they become dissatisfied with a course of therapy, even if the doctor is very good. You're correct, though. It is disappointing to see them leave prematurely."

Heather's deadpan was excellent; Lauren would never have guessed that Sabrina Andersen was now a steady patient of Heather's boss. Lauren would have congratulated her on her professionalism if Heather's wealth of discretion wasn't lousing up her plans.

Lauren sighed. "It's getting late. We'd better get you back to the office."

As Lauren drove back to her own office it was clear that the only way she was going to get at the psychiatrist's records was through a court order. The police could get one, but only after she brought in enough evidence to make Sabrina Andersen a murder suspect. For now, she was going to forget about Dr.

Ferris and go on what she'd learned from observing Sabrina firsthand and from Bill's interview with her.

Back in her office, she was just wondering whether it was worth noting in the file that she'd lunched with Heather when Bill sauntered in. There was a small red stain on his gray tie, probably marinara sauce, and he wore the satisfied mug of a well-fed tomcat. "Been keeping busy?" he asked.

"Yes, more productively than you have." Though not by much, she thought ruefully.

Bill blissfully ignored the gibe as he folded himself into a chair.

Despite his annoyingly happy mood, she felt an overwhelming desire to share her frustration with him. Giving in, she said, "Over lunch I tried to find out about Sabrina's psychiatric records."

"From whom?"

"Dr. Ferris."

He looked blank.

"Her shrink," Lauren prompted. "Remember?" Had he been paying any attention to the case, or was his mind always on women?

Bill's right brow rose in question. "You're telling me you had lunch with Dr. Ferris?"

Lauren slumped a little. "No, not him—his secretary. I'm afraid it was a waste of time," she conceded.

Bill ran a hand over his forehead; his eyes were full of mirth. "Well, in that case, I've got some news that may please you."

She sensed he was teasing her again. Whatever was up his sleeve, she wasn't going to react this time. "They've arrested Sabrina?" she said dryly.

"Good guess, but no."

She leaned back and crossed her knees with an air of bored impatience. "I give up."

"I just had lunch with Ferris."

"Dr. Ferris?"

Bill's mouth threatened to twist into a smirk, then righted itself. "Yes, Tim's an old college buddy of mine, a fellow Irishman. We met at Santa Rosa JC."

"I see." Her mind was reeling, even as her cheeks felt warm and pink. Damn it, he'd gotten her again! She reminded herself of her wasted time trying to pry information out of the doctor's receptionist. "Why didn't you tell me last night that you knew him?"

Bill's smile faded and he shrugged. "I tried to. I offered to talk to Ferris for you, but you interrupted me and said there was something else you wanted me to do."

"That's no excuse." Lauren was really angry. "You could have told me this morning, instead of letting me waste my time and money with his secretary. We're supposed to be working together on this. And you still haven't explained where you were this morning."

"I was tracking Tim down. He was out running with his personal trainer. I ended up having to wait at his house for him to return, and then he was in a rush to get to the office, so I made the lunch date with him." He paused a moment, finally looking contrite. "I'm sorry I didn't tell you. If I'd realized you were planning to interview his secretary, I would have told you."

Lauren was still a little disconcerted, but his apology made her feel better. She started to give him a lecture about not letting it happen again, then decided it would probably be more effective to spit in the wind. She waved one hand. "So tell me what you found out from Ferris. Was he very forthcoming?"

"Yes. Lucky thing he owed me one. He says Sabrina is a typical major depressive, nothing more, nothing less. She's been that way for about ten years, since the initial onset of the depression when she was in college. She's been his patient for approximately two years. He says he's prescribed some mild sleeping pills, but no other drugs."

"I see. Did he mention schizophrenia or any other psychological or mood disorder?"

"No," Bill said emphatically.

Lauren pursed her lips. "How often does he see Sabrina?"

"Once a week, sometimes twice if she's having a particularly bad time."

Lauren raised her eyebrows. "Nat said she was there all the time. Are you sure Ferris was telling you the truth?"

"Yes, I'm sure! Tim's a very straight guy. I don't think he would even have talked to me if her case wasn't so straightforward and I hadn't promised to keep it confidential. He wouldn't lie to me."

"Okay. But even if he was giving you his true opinion, psychiatry is an inexact science," she said, quoting Dr. Hosmer. "Sometimes even the best doctors miss a diagnosis."

Bill shook his head in disgust, then leaned back with one finger stiffly supporting his jaw. A brittle light flashed in the depths of his brown eyes. After a moment he said, "You're really determined to pin this on Sabrina Andersen, aren't you? Are you sure your personal feelings aren't getting in the way?"

Lauren's eyes flew open in genuine surprise. "I don't know what you're talking about," she said. But she did know; he was implying again that she'd had a thing for Nat Andersen. She'd thought that issue was behind them, and all this time he'd been harboring a sleazy opinion of her. No wonder he'd thought he could steal a kiss in the front seat of his car!

The roller-coaster ride her emotions had been on all week made her temper snap. "I've got solid reasons for suspecting Sabrina, and if you weren't so intent on disagreeing with me and being a maverick, you'd see them, too." Lauren's hand shot out and she began ticking off her fingers. "One, the woman has been under a psychiatrist's care, and many of the symptoms of major depression are similar to those of schizophrenia, which typically has its onset in young adulthood, just the time Sabrina first became ill. You yourself heard Dr. Hosmer say that in some cases schizophrenics are capable of violence.

"Number two, Sabrina sought out Nat and me in the restaurant and threatened us. Number three, she had access to the limousine the night of the murder. Number four, three days after Nat was killed, I was attacked by a woman lying in wait for me. The woman's height and build perfectly match Sabrina's.

"And finally, Nat Andersen was a decent, considerate, kind man. The reason he hired me, which you didn't need to know to fulfill your assignment, was to pose as his girlfriend to give his wife grounds for divorce, so her family would put the blame on Nat, not her, for the breakup. I *know* from spending several days with Nat that he wasn't the kind of man who attracts enemies, and the police haven't turned up anyone with a motive for murdering him."

Bill looked unimpressed. "I think you spent *too much* time with Andersen, Lauren." His lips wrinkled in distaste. "The man totally charmed you. Do you really believe that story he gave you about wanting you to play his girlfriend so he could get a divorce? That's a fairy tale if ever I heard one!" Bill's voice became husky. "The truth is, you were in love with him, weren't you?

"I've dealt with a lot of lowlifes in my time," he continued firmly, "and this Andersen was definitely a scumbag. He had you completely buffaloed. I don't know what kind of dirt he was into or who he crossed enough to make that person kill him, but I'm going to find out."

She was preparing a retort when the phone rang. "Yes!" she snapped, picking up the receiver.

"Uh, sorry to interrupt," Julie said, "but it's private investigator Phillip Cameron, returning your call. Do you want to take it?"

It was her Orange County contact. Lauren straightened in her chair and lowered her voice to a confidential tone. "Yes, I will. Thanks." There was a click, and Lauren said, "Phil? Hi. Thanks for getting back to me."

"No problem, especially when the assignment's this easy."

Lauren's eyes flicked to Bill.

"You're familiar with the man I asked you about?" she said into the phone.

"Sure, Donelan is well-known down here. His uncle started a one-man agency in downtown L.A. in the late seventies. Bill joined forces with him about ten years ago and built the agency up to six or eight full-time dicks. The uncle had a heart attack, oh, about four years ago. Since then he's been living on the golf course and Bill's had full charge. I think they had some kind of bust-up—the old codger wasn't a real joy to get along with—so Bill put the word out he was moving back up your way to start his own shop."

"He was from this area originally?"

"Yeah. Petaluma's right near you, isn't it? I think he was a cop there in the early eighties, before quitting the force and coming to L.A."

Lauren groaned. Bill had more experience than she could shake a stick at.

"Anything else?"

"No. Thanks, Phil. I appreciate it."

Lauren hung up the phone in a daze. All this time Bill Donelan had let her think he was a tenderfoot when he was actually a skilled, cunning professional.

Lord, why hadn't she called Phil earlier, last week, when she first grew suspicious? She wanted to deny Bill was out to hurt her, wanted to tell herself it wasn't true. But how else could she explain the facts? And she'd introduced him to Ed Ramsey and given him a list of many of her best contacts!

She thought she'd maintained a neutral expression while she digested the call, but Bill asked, "Are you okay?"

"Yes." The man had a way of reading her moods that was uncanny! Her only chance was to make him confess the truth, to intimidate him so he wouldn't think he could steal her contacts. But she'd have to make it convincing, or he'd guess how unnerved she was.

She steepled her fingers in hard points before her and made her tone dry. "Strange how you never bothered to tell me about your background, Bill. Quite an accomplishment, building up your uncle's firm like that." She felt a bead of sweat trickle between her shoulder blades.

Bill found himself momentarily lost by her change in subject. He shifted in his chair and squinted at her. "Who was that on the phone?"

"An old acquaintance of yours. Phillip Cameron," she said. Her beautiful eyes had turned to gray steel.

Bill kicked himself. Damn! He should have taken the trouble to set her straight about himself, instead of letting it go. Still, it was the woman's own fault for brushing off his early attempts to explain. It made him mad.

"I would have told you if you let me," he said. "If the news comes as a shock, I'm afraid I can't help it."

"Can't help the fact that you deceived me?" She snorted. "And you were the one who pretended to care so much about ethics."

They glared at one another for a moment. Women were difficult, but he'd never met one worse than this! He was sorely tempted to walk out and let her mangle the Andersen case all by herself.

Lauren stood and rested her knuckles on the desk top. "Since I can't trust you, keeping you on is out of the question." Her gaze faltered, but she forced her eyes up to meet his. "You're fired."

Bill's complexion darkened to a deep red and his neck swelled at his collar. "Good," he said, rising and slamming his fist down on the desk under her nose. "That's just fine with me! And may the best investigator win! We'll see who solves this case and gets the job with the district attorney!"

Chapter Eight

Lauren spent the night tossing and turning. The scene with Bill replayed itself again and again like a waking nightmare—first his fist crashing down on her desk and his threat to wrest from her the D.A.'s job, then her hands flying to her face, feeling as though she'd been physically slapped.

"You wouldn't," she'd said in a hushed voice. "Ramsey offered that job to *me*."

"Wrong again. He offered it to the P.I. who can bring in evidence leading to an arrest and conviction." He'd smiled maliciously as he waved one hand in an arc. "See you around, sweetheart." Then he'd sauntered out, slamming the door behind him.

Lauren rose early the next morning, feeling exhausted, and left for the office at six, afraid she might accidentally run into Bill in the hall if she arrived any later. But it was almost eight when she heard Bill's office door open and close. Her hands paused for a fraction of a second on the computer keys, and she told herself it didn't matter that he was next door, working against her for the D.A.'s job. But deceiving herself became impossible.

She buried her aching forehead in her hands. Why, oh why, had she ever trusted that man to help her? She'd introduced him to Ramsey, taken him onto the Andersen estate, given him the lead on Dr. Ferris.... Talk about jump-starting his investigation! What was wrong with her? If she lost this appointment with the D.A., she'd have to close the agency. There was no question of that now. She'd not only be letting her father down, she'd be putting Julie out on the street at a time when jobs were almost impossible to find, even for those with excellent skills.

How had her ability to judge people, to read their real motives, gone so wrong? How could she have become romantically attracted to a man who would take advantage of her like that?

That was the real problem, the reason she felt so uncharacteristically despairing and powerless. She had fallen for Bill. If this had been only a matter of business, she would have been enraged, determined to whip him. Instead, she felt miserable because she couldn't stop wanting him.

She reached in her desk drawer for a tissue. The one thing she would not let him do was make her cry. Crying was for funerals. The last time she'd cried was at her father's graveside. She would cry for the loss of a loved one, but not for the closing of her business, and certainly not for the part of her foolish heart that seemed to be breaking.

Julie came in and called out a greeting, apologizing for being late. Lauren blew her nose. It was past eight; she should start making those calls she'd set aside the day before.

She spent the rest of the morning on the phone, stalwartly seeking medical records for the Falletti family. She wasn't able to get any information from Sabrina's private physician; but her contact in the records department at Santa Rosa Memorial Hospital did better with Sabrina's parents. Apparently Mrs. Falletti had been seen twice in the hospital emergency room for stitches: once in the leg and hand, once in the temple. Lauren found that particularly interesting.

Her contact was also able to get some information from the staff in the office of the senior Fallettis' personal doctor: nothing in their charts indicated a family history of schizophrenia, but he had prescribed sleeping pills for the mother.

With each call, Lauren casually asked if anyone else had inquired about the Falletti family. She was relieved when the responses were all negative; Bill still had the contact list she'd given him, but at least he wasn't using it yet.

Right after lunch she drove across the Bay to the UC Berkeley campus and obtained a copy of Sabrina's university transcript. That, combined with a visit to the sorority house where Sabrina had lived, revealed that Sabrina had stayed in school only a year and a half before dropping out to marry Nat Andersen. She'd been less social than other girls in Phi Gamma Theta, but the housemistress remembered Sabrina's roommates: a Sonoma girl with the married name of Irene Trevino, and Mary Campbell, a Marylander. Lauren carefully noted the names of the two women. One of them might have witnessed the beginnings of Sabrina's mental illness.

Back in her office, Lauren set the wheels in motion to track down Irene Trevino and then called a fellow P.I. in Baltimore to give him Mary Campbell's last known address. He promised to look for Campbell and call Lauren back as soon as he located her.

Her final incoming call of the day was from the detective she'd hired to surveil Sabrina. He didn't have much to report; Mark Andersen was the only person who'd been off the estate all day.

WHEN BILL ARRIVED at his office building the following morning, he told himself it didn't matter if he ran into Lauren or not, but nonetheless he felt relieved when he stepped off the elevator and didn't see her.

The things he'd said to her two days ago made him feel like a cad, but apologizing for them wouldn't solve his problems with her, not while she was still slavishly devoted to Nat Andersen's memory. Andersen had been rich, good-looking and unhappily married—the kind women were always falling over. Naturally when he turned up dead, Lauren was sure the culprit must be the prize's jealous wife. Though Sabrina was obviously a basket case, Bill doubted the woman was a homicidal maniac. When he couldn't go along with

Lauren's theory and suggested Andersen could be to blame for his own death, she'd hit the roof.

If he tried to make amends with Lauren, she'd demand he stop investigating Andersen and help her pin it on Sabrina. But he couldn't do that. He had a feeling there was something much deeper to all this than just a case of wifely jealousy. If he apologized and then told Lauren he wouldn't help her, she'd think he was talking out of both sides of his mouth.

No, the only course was for him to concentrate on the task at hand: exposing Nat. The best thing he could do for Lauren was prove that Andersen had been lying to her and using her. Nothing else would break her infatuation.

He quickly let himself into his office and turned on the lights. He had an appointment to interview Chuck Caine this morning, but there was one call he wanted to make first. The nagging feeling of guilt began to fade as he sat down at his desk and pulled the phone toward himself.

Flipping through his Rolodex, he found the number of a woman he'd affectionately nicknamed Auntie Mame. While the phone rang, his mind flicked over the work he'd done on the case over the past two days. He'd checked out Nat Andersen's bank and credit records, his school, service and police records. Nothing wrong there. He'd spent several hours with all the back newspaper articles on Andersen and Micom but found nothing provocative. Even the union rep he spoke with sang Andersen's praises! Micom offered the best wages and benefits in the industry. Though its owner was known for ruthlessly cutting out the competition, his own people were as loyal to him as cocker spaniels. But if there was a chink in Nat's suit of shining armor, Bill was going to find it.

A soft-spoken woman answered the phone. The voice was familiar, but not the tone.

"Ada, is that you?" Bill said. "You won't believe this, but I can hardly hear you."

"Yes, this is Ada Levine." The woman's voice rose in volume with each word until Bill was forced to hold the receiver away from his ear.

"That's much better," he told her. "I was afraid for a moment you were sick. How are you?"

"I'm just fine, except that you woke me. Who is this?"

"It's Bill Donelan, Ada. It's been a long time. Are you still living in that Victorian relic on McDonald Avenue?"

"Yes, I'm still here, you nasty boy," Ada replied with enthusiasm, "and I *adore* this old Victorian. They'll have to bury me in the rose garden. It's good to hear from you. Are you back from Los Angeles?"

"Yes, I am."

Bill heard a double click on the line and Ada said, "Oh, I have another call coming in. Do you mind waiting?"

Ada punched a button on her phone. "Hello?"

"Ada? This is Lauren Pierce. How are you?"

"Lauren, my dear, how nice of you to call. You shouldn't be such a stranger. Your dear father used to call me all the time! How are you? Charming and beautiful as ever?''

Sitting at her desk, the phone to her ear, Lauren smiled. "I'm well, Ada. Thanks for asking."

"How is your mother these days?"

"She's just fine, and my sister is getting married next month. The ceremony will be in the chapel at the Luther Burbank Center." Lauren went on to give her all the details, knowing Ada would relish them.

"How splendid, Lauren. Please give Susan my congratulations. She's such a perky little thing. I wish her all the best. Listen, my friend Bill has been holding on the other line. Would you mind waiting while I get back to him for a moment?"

Lauren blanched. "Bill? That wouldn't be Bill Donelan, by any chance?"

"Yes, you're right. I'll get right back to you."

"Ada! Don't tell him—"

But Ada had already switched lines. Lauren whisked the phone off her desk and carried it into the passage, glaring at the connecting door between her office and Bill's.

Bill tilted the receiver to his mouth as Ada came back on the line.

"So, what were you saying, Bill? You promised you'd return to Santa Rosa one day."

"Yes, though it took me longer than expected. I've opened my own private-detective agency on Fourth Street. I thought you might be able to tell me something about one of our late, local celebrities."

"Of course, dear, though you know how little I listen to gossip."

"Uh-huh." Bill grinned.

"I'll wager I can guess who it is you want to know about. Nat Andersen?"

"I'm impressed."

"It's really nothing, my dear Watson," she said with a flourish. "No one else who matters a fig has died in Santa Rosa in the last month, knock on wood." Bill heard the faint sound of knuckles rapping. "So, what would you like to know?"

"Tell me about his personal life, his reputation with the ladies."

"Very dull—unusually so, for a man with a wife like Sabrina Falletti. I've never heard a breath of any sort of scandal, or even a dalliance, from that quarter. He's not at all the ladies' man his brother Mark is, who I hear is back in town and still unmarried. I'm sorry."

Bill inwardly felt disappointed, but kept silent. Ada's call-waiting clicked again.

"Did you have something else to ask me?" she said. "I'll have to put you on hold for a minute, because I've got Lauren on the other line."

"Lauren?" Bill shot up straight in his chair. "Is she calling about Nat, too?"

"She hasn't told me yet. Hold on." Pause. "Lauren, forgive me for keeping you. What can I do for you?"

"Did you tell Bill I was on the other line?"

"Yes, dear. Was that all right?"

Lauren slumped against the wall of the reception area and folded her arm with the phone across her breasts. "Yes, it's no problem." She sighed. "What did he want?"

"He's been asking me about Nat Andersen."

"Mmm. I'm not surprised."

"Yes, he wanted to know about Nat's affairs of the heart. I'm afraid I disappointed him. Nat was a saint."

Lauren smiled with satisfaction. She hoped the blank wall Ada threw up in front of Bill had flattened his nose.

"I agree," Lauren said. "I knew Nat slightly, and I never thought he was unfaithful to his wife. Actually it's Sabrina Andersen I'm calling you about."

"How interesting. Well, you probably know Sabrina's off in the head. Has been since before she married Nat. Too much of her father's cheap wine as an infant? No, that's unkind. Forget I said that."

"Is Sabrina's problem only depression, or do you think it's something more?" Lauren probed, phrasing the question as discreetly as she could.

"I don't know, probably just a predisposition to melancholy."

"Does she have any friends around town? Who does she socialize with?"

"I don't think she goes out very much. I know she's not involved in any of the local charities or women's groups—even those popular twelve-step programs everyone belongs to. I never see Sabrina out unless she's with Nat in some restaurant. Now, I suppose, she'll have nothing to keep her from being a total recluse."

"Can you think of anyone at all she might be close to? Someone who might have regular contact with her?"

"No, other than her mother, who is a real... I won't say the word, but you get my drift. An unpleasant woman, very high in the instep, as the English used to say. All the Fallettis are that way."

"Have you heard of any violent tendencies in the family?"

"Violence? No. Pathological cussedness, yes. The mother is an alcoholic, been in and out of the drug-rehabilitation program up in Pope Valley, but I can't think of anything along the lines you're referring to."

Lauren exhaled. "I guess that's all I wanted to ask. Thank you, as always."

"Don't mention it, my dear. We'll have to talk again soon. Goodbye."

Bill thrummed his fingers against the chair arm as he waited for Ada. If he opened the window he could probably eavesdrop on her conversation with Lauren.

"Bill, are you still there? You faithful man! I'm sorry to keep you so long."

"No problem." He wasn't going to bother asking Ada about her other caller; in her crusade to frame Sabrina, Lauren had probably posed all the wrong questions, anyway.

"What have you heard about Nat's company, Micom, Inc.?" Bill asked. "Anything amiss there?"

"Hmm... I don't think so. You know, of course, about that new computer of theirs, the one that listens to you." She chuckled. "But I've never heard of anything irregular connected with the firm. Nat was very polished. He always said the right thing and his manners were impeccable. That's about the only thing I could say against him. Someone that good could take a shortcut or two and you'd never notice it.

"So," she continued with barely a pause, "now that I've helped you, dear boy, *you* must tell *me* what you're after. He really was murdered, wasn't he?"

"I'm sorry, I can't say."

Ada sighed loudly. "I knew you'd say that. But you don't have to tell me. I can draw my own conclusions when two private eyes call me in the same morning. Speaking of Lauren, where did you say your office was? Fourth Street? You must be quite near her. If you're both investigating the Andersens, you should get together."

"My thought exactly," Bill conceded, "but if you know Lauren, you know she's stubborn."

Ada chortled. "You're right. But something tells me you're more than a match for her, Bill. I've got to run. Promise you'll meet me for lunch soon. I'll call you."

Bill hung up the receiver, flopped back in his desk chair and flicked his tie with one hand.

Ada was right, one hundred percent. This feud between him and Lauren was ridiculous. Here they were, practically sitting in each other's laps, duplicating one another's work. What a waste of time! If Ada had known the true situation, she would have laughed at them for a couple of clowns.

Bill vaulted out of his chair. It was time someone talked some sense into Lauren Pierce, and like Ada had said, he was the man to do it!

LAUREN HUNG UP after speaking with Ada and stared at the connecting door, mentally sending darts Bill Donelan's way. She carried the phone back into her office and was setting it on the desk when the front door opened.

"I'm Mark Andersen," the visitor told Julie. "I'd like to speak with Ms. Pierce."

Nat's brother? Had he changed his mind about the death being an accident? She stepped out to greet him.

Mark Andersen was shorter than his brother had been, but their hair coloring was the same pale yellow, and the facial resemblance was almost disconcerting. Lauren hid her shock as she extended her hand and said calmly, "I'm Lauren Pierce. It's a pleasure to meet you, Mr. Andersen. Won't you come in?"

She closed the door behind them, then took her seat, saying, "I was very sorry to hear about your brother's death. It's a terrible tragedy."

Andersen waved aside her sympathetic preamble. "I'll get right to the point, Ms. Pierce. My sister-in-law told me about the 'insurance investigator' who visited her yesterday. I believe you were driving as I passed him on his way out. Knowing my brother had no policy with any company named Security Life, I contacted the sheriff's department and told them someone was trying to interview Sabrina under false pretenses. The deputy told me that you had appeared at their office, inquiring about Nat's death, and that you might be responsible for the ruse."

Lauren wondered who Mark Andersen had spoken to at the sheriff's office. Had he wrestled poor Ed Ramsey to the mat, or had one of the jealous lieutenants found out about her?

She kept her gaze steady and unapologetic as she answered, "Yes, I'm working alongside the sheriff's department."

"Ms. Pierce, I think you're lying. If you had their authorization, your man wouldn't have needed a pretext to speak to my sister-in-law. I don't like having my family lied to, especially Sabrina. This is hard enough for her as it is."

OUT IN THE RECEPTION AREA, Bill paced as he waited for Lauren to get free.

The sound of raised voices penetrated Lauren's door. Julie looked up and Bill frowned. "Who's she got in there?" he asked.

Julie's brows narrowed in concern. "Mark Andersen. He looked ready to spit when he went in. I hope everything's all right."

Lauren was unsuccessfully trying to calm her angry visitor when she saw the door behind his standing figure open and Bill Donelan walk in.

"Excuse me for interrupting, Lauren, but I heard our client's brother was here and I'd like to meet him."

Andersen swung around. "Are you the one who was sneaking around our house?"

Bill's crooked smile said, *Aren't you exaggerating a bit, old boy?* "Yes, I'm Bill Donelan." He held out his hand.

Mark ignored it, and Bill crossed his arms. "Mr. Andersen, it's true we used a pretext to speak to your sister-in-law," he said calmly, "but it was in the interest of learning the truth of what happened to your brother. I can assure you our only motive for investigating this case is to bring Nat's murderer to justice."

Mark snapped, "It has *not* been demonstrated my brother was murdered. Besides, you can't fool me. I don't know whether the pair of you want to sell some fabricated story to one of those television news shows or write your own bestseller, but I want it to stop here!" He leaned over Lauren's desk and slammed his right fist into his left palm.

Bill stepped between them, but Lauren didn't flinch. Her eyes were luminous with disbelief. "You can't honestly believe it was an accident! The brakes suddenly failing, the phony telephone call from his plant—"

"Coincidences! My family is working with the police to get this matter settled as quickly and quietly as possible. We've cooperated in every way with the sheriff's detectives, and I am completely satisfied with the job they're doing. We've already had too much publicity. I won't let you turn this into a scandal."

Lauren scowled. "Mr. Andersen, what *I* see is a set of very suspicious circumstances, and we owe it to Nat not to rest until we find out what really happened."

Mark stepped threateningly toward her. Lauren drew back in her chair, but Bill had him by the lapels and dragged him back like a rag doll.

Seeing the fury in Bill's face, she was sure he was about to throttle the other man. She scrambled to her feet. "Bill, don't!" Bill threw her a look that said, *Be quiet and let me handle this,* but he loosened his hold on Mark.

"If you want to threaten people, Andersen, then listen close." He let go and Mark stumbled back. "Nat was our client, and he hired Ms. Pierce to pose as his girlfriend so that Sabrina would offer him a divorce and so she could tell her family the breakup was all hubby's fault. You want a scandal? I could blurt that around town and you'd have one. We don't need to fabricate a story for the *National Enquirer*—we've already got one! And if you don't believe me, just raise your voice to Ms. Pierce once more."

Lauren tried to take some heat out of the situation. "We're really not interested in extortion. Nat died owing me six hundred dollars, and I haven't approached you for that, have I?"

Mark Andersen's face had fallen into a miasma of dismay. He avoided Bill's dilated eyes and Lauren's shuttered blue ones. After a moment, he pulled a checkbook and pen from his inside coat pocket and quickly wrote a check.

Lauren resumed her seat as he tore it off and tossed it onto her desk. "I believe that settles Nat's account."

"Yes, but not this case," Lauren said as she placed the check in her middle desk drawer. Behind Mark, Bill was smiling. She folded her hands on top of the oak surface. "Thank you."

Bill beamed at her as Andersen beat a hasty retreat. When he was gone, Lauren blew out her cheeks. "My word, what an idiot! Did he think I was blackmailing him there at the end? I've got the time cards and invoice to prove it."

Bill leaned back against the doorjamb. "Don't worry about it. Six hundred bucks is small change to those bastards. He knows a blackmailer would ask for a lot more."

"I can't believe he's related to Nat," Lauren thought out loud. "They look like twins, yet Mark acts as though his family name is more important than the stolen life of his brother. I'm sure Nat wouldn't have responded that way if it had been Mark who'd mysteriously died."

Bill snorted. He hadn't stirred from his post. As she looked up, the memory of what had passed between them suddenly returned like a flood. Her pulse had leapt when he first appeared, but incredible as it seemed, she'd forgotten her fight with Bill in the flush of dueling beside him with Mark.

The thought that he'd come to her aid threatened to warm her heart. She pushed the dangerous sentiment aside. She couldn't allow him to affect her that way again. She had to find out what he wanted and send him away.

"What brings you here?" she said coldly.

The corners of Bill's mouth turned down. "That three-ring circus with Ada."

Lauren said nothing, but he could tell from the tick beside one of her Siamese-like eyes that she knew he'd been on the other phone line.

He parted his jacket to rest his hands on his belt. "It's ridiculous, the two of us working against each other on this. Surely you can see that."

Lauren lowered her eyes and shook her head. She couldn't see anything right now. It was taking all her concentration not to let the pain in her chest overwhelm her.

"Is that your last silence on it?" Bill said, trying to make her laugh.

Lauren sat numbly, staring at her desk.

Bill glared at his watch and pushed himself away from the door. "Damn it. You won't see reason. I'm tempted to just throw you over my shoulder and drag you along with me today!"

Lauren's chin came up. "Just try it!"

For a second, she thought he might. He looked frustrated enough to try anything. He wrinkled his nose and shot a warning finger at her. "I've got to go, but we'll settle this when I get back."

As he turned on his heel, an inner voice cried out to Lauren to stop him, that letting him go would be agony. She could wait for him to return, to see him once more, but the hours would seem like days.

Longing forced strength into her legs. She stood and shouted at his back, "Where are you going?"

"To Caine Industries to interview Chuck Caine."

She ignored the fading voice of caution in her head and flew around the desk. "I'm going with you."

Bill's jaw sagged as he watched her shrug into her raincoat. "I thought you didn't want to have anything to do with me."

"I don't," Lauren said, self-consciously hitching her purse strap over her shoulder. "But I, uh, don't trust you, either. If you're going to learn something from Caine, I want to hear every word."

Chapter Nine

They spoke little as Bill took the two-lane back road out of Santa Rosa, heading for neighboring Rohnert Park and the Caine Industries complex.

Lauren kept her eyes on the fallow fields lining the road as she pondered exactly what she'd gotten herself into.

The first few minutes of the coming interview were guaranteed to be ticklish when Caine recognized her as the woman he'd seen Nat with at Pebble Beach. She'd have to explain why Nat had hired her and try to convince Caine that Nat had had Sabrina's best interests in mind when he pretended to be having an affair.

Sitting beside her, Bill was absorbed in his own thoughts. He was relieved they were working together again, and he'd agreed to take her to Caine because Nat's competitor might well be able to convince her if there was something underhand going on at Micom. However, taking Lauren in to the interview would pose some real problems.

"Lauren," he began tentatively, "I want to include you in this, but for the sake of the investigation, I think it might be better if I went in to see Caine alone. You see, Caine is expecting me to be a reporter for a computer magazine, and if we go in together and he recognizes you, it'll blow my cover and probably our chances of getting any information from him."

Though she agreed with his logic, she eyed him suspiciously. "How do I know that's your real reason for wanting to go alone?"

"Because I'm telling you the honest truth, damn it!"

Bill pulled the Taurus onto the dirt shoulder and rolled to a stop.

"What are you doing?" Lauren asked. Was he going to forcibly eject her from the car?

"We're going to settle this now, once and for all," he said with grim determination. He shut off the engine and turned to face her, his left arm braced on the steering wheel. "That stuff I said about competing with you for the D.A.'s job was a lot of bull."

Lauren moved her knee from where it touched his and scrunched back against the door. She raised one brow archly.

"I was mad," he continued, "because you got so ticked at me and because I felt like an idiot for not making it clear to you who I was. I knew if I threatened your job with the D.A. it would get your goat, but I didn't for one second mean it."

When she looked stubbornly unconvinced, he ran his hand through his hair. "Haven't you ever said something in the heat of the moment and almost instantly regretted it?"

Lauren ignored the question. "That doesn't explain why you didn't tell me about your experience in L.A."

The corners of Bill's mouth turned downward. "As I said before, I tried to. That afternoon in the hall, when you griped about my door sign, I told you I hadn't graduated from that fly-by-night correspondence school. Remember?"

Bill waited. It was like pulling teeth, but Lauren finally said, "Yes."

"And the next time I saw you, when you hired me to tail you and Nat, I tried to tell you then, but you shut me up and said you didn't want to know."

Lauren's eyes fell. "I was afraid you weren't licensed and I was embarrassed I couldn't get someone more qualified to work with me."

"After that, I thought to hell with her. If she's determined to treat me like a rookie, let her. I knew it wouldn't take long with us working together for you to realize you'd made a mistake and ask me about my background, but you never did."

Lauren gave a guilty little grimace. He was right. She should have asked him herself. "That's one possible explanation of your motive for not telling me," she said, "but where's the proof?"

Bill let the air escape from his lungs and his head dropped. He pinched the bridge of his nose, then spread his forefinger and thumb to his closed lids.

When he looked up again, his eyes were filled with an aching sincerity.

"You want to know how I really feel about all this, Lauren? You've worked in this town a lot longer than I have, and if I can help you get that D.A.'s job, I will. You deserve it. The last thing in the world I want is to sabotage your getting it."

Lauren felt deeply confused. Was it only her desire to believe him that made her feel he was being honest, or was it her sound P.I.'s instinct? Could any man be this good an actor? She faltered, reaching out to the only person she could for guidance. "How do I know you're telling the truth?"

"This way," he said. His big hands slid around her shoulders; he gently pulled her close and kissed her.

Her hands came up to his chest to push him away, but her willpower faded as he held her fast in his arms and his lips coaxed hers to respond. Her bones turned to milk where he touched her and the strength left her arms. Lord how she wanted this. She wanted *him!*

His tongue probed gently at the seam of her lips. She waited for him to demand, to force his way past her resistance, but he held back, returned to kissing her with just his lips. The next time he ran the tip of his tongue over her mouth she gave in, opening to him, absorbing him, reveling in him.

The man was a superb kisser. The best. Her heart ached to show him how she felt, to throw all of herself into her caresses, but she dared not. And when he pulled slightly away from her, she let him go.

They sat starring into one another's eyes for a moment, Lauren trying to read what was in his heart. She saw desire in the dark mahogany depths, but was there anything deeper, more spiritual, in his feelings for her? She'd thought she felt the stirrings of deeper emotions in his kiss, but she couldn't be sure.

Lauren turned her head and gazed sightlessly out the windshield. One thing she *was* sure of was Bill Donelan's ambition. If he used her, made love to her and then betrayed her, he must know the other P.I.'s in town would hear of it, and his chances of building a business in Santa Rosa would be ruined. She grew certain that was something he'd never do.

She cleared her throat but didn't pull back from where his right hand still rested on her shoulder. "How do you propose we work together?"

A light leapt in Bill's eyes. "Just coordinate with me so we can pool what information we gather. You don't have to introduce me to any more of your sources if you don't feel comfortable doing it. In fact—" he fished inside his inner jacket pocket and pulled out a sheet "—I think this belongs to you."

Lauren unfolded her contact list. There were no marks on it; it appeared pristine, as though it had never left his jacket pocket since she saw him place it there two mornings ago.

She considered it silently for a moment, then said, "I trust you."

An almost boyish gratification and thankfulness suffused Bill's rugged face. Lowering his head, he tenderly brushed her lips once more.

The kiss was so sweet, his manner so forthcoming, that she felt a tickle of guilt in her ribs. "Bill," she said, scooting back as he released her, "I have a confession to make, too. I'm sorry I didn't tell you the real reason Nat hired me when I asked you to surveil us. I was afraid you wouldn't understand, so I didn't tell you I was hired to pose as his girlfriend. Then, when I began to suspect you were jealous, well, it flattered me. When you came by my house to show me the newspaper, I should have explained right then and there that I wasn't attracted to Nat, not in the least. When you saw me fawning on him in the restaurant, it was all an act. Nat didn't even want to touch me, but I told him he should or he'd never fool anyone that he cared for me."

Bill's eyes widened. "Why you little..." He threw his head back and guffawed, holding the bottom of the wheel as he shook. The hearty sound was infectious, and Lauren started laughing, too.

"Oh, Lord, I think we've been in this business too long," he said, wiping his eyes. "We're so used to deceiving people in the pursuit of truth that we don't know when to stop. Speaking of which," he said, checking his watch, "I'm nearly thirty minutes late for my covert interview. Think Caine will believe I'm a reporter?"

Lauren starting laughing again. "I think he'd believe you were the sultan of Brunei if you told him."

"Thank you. I'll take that as a professional compliment. But from now on—" he looked her in the face "—you and I are straight with one another, on everything, right?"

"Right. And if you don't tell me every word Caine says, I'll karate-chop you."

He grabbed for her ribs to tickle her, and Lauren shouted, "No, no, I'm just kidding! Stop!"

It was several more minutes before the blue Taurus pulled back onto the road.

A PHONE ON the secretary's desk rang. She picked it up, then turned to Bill. "Mr. Caine will see you now."

Bill entered the spacious office and casually glanced about. A wide window that looked out on the plant provided task lighting for Caine's mahogany desk while the tan walls were in shadow; spots recessed into the ceiling illuminated old-time prints of prizefighters and racehorses. A pair of leather armchairs with brass studs stood before the desk, and a small wet bar was built into the wall by the door.

Caine rose to greet him. As he extended his hand, the gray, double-breasted suit rippled over his beefy shoulders. At first glance, Bill had estimated Caine to be nearing sixty, because he was almost bald and his fringe of dark hair was flecked with gray. But a luxuriant black mustache covered his full lips, and as Bill took his hand and looked into the man's forceful brown eyes, he realized Caine was probably only fifty.

"Thank you for seeing me, Mr. Caine. I'm sorry I was so late," Bill said, releasing the firm grip and stepping back.

"No problem," Caine replied briskly, indicating the chair across from his desk.

"You have quite a plant here. Very impressive."

"Yes, we're right behind Hewlett-Packard and gaining. We're the second-largest computer manufacturer north of Silicon Valley. Which magazine are you with, Mr. Hart?"

"*Computer Times.* We're doing an article on the career of Nathaniel Andersen and the future of Micom, Inc., now that he's gone."

"Yes, very tragic. He was such a young man."

Without taking his eyes from Caine's face, Bill pulled a small notebook from his inside coat pocket. "Micom has been a very successful company. How much of that success do you think should be credited directly to Andersen?"

Caine leaned forward on his desk as he considered the question. "Probably a large part. I know with my own company I like to keep my finger on the pulse on everything that's happening. I meet frequently with the people in charge of development, operations and marketing, and I keep my ear to the ground so I know what the average worker on the line is thinking and feeling about our products. I can't say about Andersen, his own people could tell you better, but I wouldn't be surprised if he did the same thing."

Bill nodded. Caine sounded like an advertisement for his own company—he was probably fishing for an article on Caine Industries. "And what would you say of Nat Andersen's reputation in the industry?" Bill asked.

"It was a good one. Micom's products are well manufactured and well marketed. They've never had labor or distribution problems. They've been a reliable company with steady, moderate growth."

"Until recently. This new product of theirs, the Micom Voice Processor 1000 that takes rapid human dictation and converts it to ASCII—it's going to make a lot of money for the company, wouldn't you say?"

"Yes, you're undoubtedly right. I wish we'd come up with it first, in fact." Caine smiled absently. "Too bad he didn't live to reap the rewards."

"I read that your own research lab has been working on a similar device."

"Yes, we've done quite a bit of toying with it, but Micom beat us to the punch. I think, though, in the coming years, we'll be able to give them a run for their money." He spread his hands. "The technology is still in its infancy."

"You're not afraid, then, of Micom cornering the market on voice processors?"

Something in Caine's face seemed to harden, but his voice remained even as he said, "We should have a similar, though better, product out within six months. Micom won't have time to corner the market. Besides—" he leaned back "—even IBM couldn't hold on to its monopoly. And now that Nat is gone, it remains to be seen what his heirs will do with the business."

"That's true. I've heard his brothers will take over the company, and they have no experience in computer manufacturing. Would you be interested in buying Micom if it goes up for sale?''

"I might be," Caine said, "but not surprisingly, the brothers aren't interested in selling. You can take my word for it." He gave Bill a small, confidential smile.

"You've already approached them about purchasing the company?"

"I didn't say that."

Bill let it drop and consulted his notebook. "I have just a few more questions. What was your opinion of Nat Andersen personally, as a friend?''

"I'm sorry, but I really didn't know him that well. We'd meet two or three times a year, at trade shows or conventions, but that was about it.''

Bill's brow wrinkled. "Are you familiar with his wife's family, the Fallettis?''

"No. I think he tried to keep his private life private, which is certainly what I do." He gave that small, confidential smile again. "But if I'd ever heard anything bad about Nat Andersen, you can be sure I'd remember it.''

LAUREN WAS WAITING for him in the parking lot. She turned off the light-rock station she'd been listening to as he climbed into the car.

"How did it go?" she asked.

"Veddy interesting, as they used to say on 'Laugh-In.'" He started the engine and gave her a word-for-word rundown of the conversation as he drove.

"It's odd," Lauren said when he'd finished, "that he denied knowing Sabrina's family.''

"Maybe Nat lied to you about that. Did Caine specifically mention Sabrina in his threat?"

"No, the only words I heard were, 'You've gone too far this time. You'll regret it.' Nat told me Caine was angry on Sabrina's behalf, and I never had reason to question his explanation."

"Maybe Caine was telling Nat he'd gone too far about something else."

"Like the voice processor?"

"Uh-huh."

Lauren thought a moment. "It could be that Caine had another motive for saying he didn't know Sabrina. It's possible he suspects Sabrina did the murder, and he doesn't want to risk incriminating her."

"Hmm. That seems less likely to me. I've done some more research on Caine in the past two days, and he's got a reputation for settling scores in a very personal way. Apparently a couple of years ago some reporter in Rohnert Park printed something untrue about Caine's company. Instead of calling his lawyer, Caine showed up at the newspaper office and decked the reporter. Last spring Caine's aides barely restrained him from taking a poke at a union leader during a contract-negotiation session."

"Jeez," Lauren said. "If Caine hadn't been at the Bohemian Club the night of the murder, I'd put him down as our prime suspect."

"I know. But there's also the problem of the mysterious woman who called Nat and lured him down the mountain, then later attacked you."

"But that was five days ago, and nothing's happened since then. Maybe the woman in the garage *was* just a vagrant."

"I'd sleep sounder at night if that was true." He reached over and squeezed her hand. "I think our next move is to dig into the rivalry between Andersen and Caine. Caine didn't try very hard to conceal his interest in acquiring Micom. Someone close to Nat must have known if Caine made an offer to buy Micom or if they argued over the development of the voice processor. I'd like to have another go at Sabrina. Maybe she's gotten her head together by now. We can talk to the driver, Dirk, again and interview the butler. He's probably well enough to talk to visitors now."

Lauren held her breath. "I'm still not prepared to clear Sabrina of suspicion."

"No, you're right. We'll keep pursuing that angle, too."

Lauren smiled. "I've tracked down an old school friend of Sabrina's, Irene Trevino. She owns a shop just a couple blocks from our offices, on lower Fourth Street, and I'd like to talk to her."

Bill nodded. "Let's get some lunch first and we'll swing over there."

There was an Italian deli in the same block as their office building. As they walked in, Lauren heard her name called.

"Laur! Over here."

"Who's that?" Bill asked.

"My sister, Suzie, and her fiancé, Allen."

They wound their way through the checkered-cloth tables, and Lauren introduced Bill.

Allen was as handsome and friendly as ever when he half rose to shake Bill's hand and buss Lauren on the cheek. Suzie was beaming, as she always seemed to be when Allen was near. Lauren choked back the familiar twinge of envy. Would she ever feel the same way as her sister? Completely happy, completely trusting in a man?

Bill and Lauren got trays and went through the line, then joined the younger couple for what turned out to be an enjoyable lunch. For the first time she learned that Bill had grown up just across town from her and attended Santa Rosa Junior College, graduating four years before she entered as a freshman. He'd even met her father once when Lawrence Pierce was working a fire insurance fraud case in Petaluma and Bill was on the police force there.

Allen had an appointment to show an office building after lunch, and the foursome walked out of the restaurant together.

"I guess it's time." Suzie sighed.

"Yes, it's time," Allen said, grinning at her.

"Time for what?" Lauren asked.

"To confess why we just happened to be having lunch next to your office," Suzie said. "The Bug broke down again this morning."

"The Volkswagen? Oh, Suzie, no! That's the second time this month. Why don't you get rid of that thing?"

"Don't discourage her, Lauren," Allen said. "I keep telling her if she's penniless by the wedding day she'll have to marry me."

"I will *not*. Sylvester Stallone is going to come for me the night before the wedding, and I *will* stand you up."

Allen didn't look amused, but Lauren smiled at the running joke. "Let's hope Stallone drives a Beetle," she whispered loudly to Allen.

"Ooh, you're ganging up on me," Suzie said, pouting. "No fair. But Bill's on my side, aren't you?" She linked arms with him.

Bill laughed. "Keep me out of this."

Lauren pulled a face. "I won't say anything more about your car, just so long as you don't ask to borrow any money to get it fixed."

"No," Suzie said, "Allen's taking care of that. What I need from you is to borrow your car. Or better yet, come with me. I'm going for the final fitting of my gown."

"I offered to take her—" Allen began.

"But I'm not letting him within a mile of that store," Suzie interrupted. "Seeing the dress before the wedding is major bad luck."

"Don't worry," Lauren said. "I wouldn't dream of endangering your future. But I can't go with you—Bill and I have got work to do." She turned to Bill. "We can take your car, can't we?"

"Sure. It's right here."

Lauren disengaged the keys to her Tercel from her ring and handed them to Suzie. "You know where I always park it."

Her sister waved goodbye as she and Bill climbed into his Ford.

ALLEN HELD Suzie's hand as they walked to the parking garage. Suzie chattered happily but he didn't say much. She knew he was probably thinking about his upcoming business appointment, so she didn't mind. He was doing so well at work that they were going to start looking for a house to buy as soon as they were married.

When they reached Lauren's car he kissed her warmly, caressing her short hair. It was getting harder to say goodbye to him with each passing day, but the thought that he was coming over for dinner in a few hours soothed her, and she remembered her fitting. "I've got to run."

She was thinking about her headpiece as she started the engine. She and the hatmaker had spent an hour working up sketches for it last week. She'd chosen a simple cap decorated with white silk roses, baby's breath and a frosting of iridescent sequins to match those on her dress. She could hardly wait to see it!

As Suzie turned right onto quiet Fifth Street, she hummed "Jesu, Joy of Man's Desiring," one of the classical pieces they'd chosen for the wedding ceremony.

A small pickup truck with a roll bar and jumbo tires was paused at the exit to a parking lot. Suzie barely noticed the stationary vehicle—she was imagining how Allen would look through the illusion netting of her veil as she floated down the aisle in her satin slippers. Suddenly there was the shriek of tires on asphalt, and the world around her caved in with a jarring thud and the shattering of glass.

As the pickup leapt across the two lanes and rammed into the driver's side of Suzie's car, the Tercel was shoved up onto the sidewalk and over a parking meter, snapping the metal stem at its base. Suzie screamed, trying frantically to escape to the other side of the car, but the seat belt held her fast as the truck's chrome bumper ground the door's armrest into her side.

Lauren's little silver car came to rest, angled up on the sidewalk, water and gasoline spurting from the undercarriage like severed arteries. Suzie screamed for help inside the grotesquely twisted vehicle as a woman with long black hair jumped from the pickup and disappeared down an alley.

Chapter Ten

Bill held the door open for Lauren as they entered Irene Trevino's dress shop. Lauren glanced around. The boutique was small, with attractive weathered-brick walls and hardwood flooring. Most of the clothing appeared to be pricey women's sportswear, some of it displayed in antique armoires. A selection of marked-down wool sweaters was neatly folded on a Queen Anne table; Lauren paused to look at them as she determined that she and Bill were the only customers. Toward the back of the shop, a woman in a plum-colored dress was attaching sale tags to a pile of items.

"You want to browse around while I talk to her?" Lauren whispered.

"Sure, honey," Bill said, speaking in a normal tone. "Take your time and look around. It's our day off."

He was only playing a part, but as she slowly made her way through the shop, Lauren thought how nice it would be if she *was* married, spending a lazy afternoon lunching and window-shopping with her husband. She imagined tugging someone like Bill by the hand into a shop like this, and him good-naturedly agreeing to wait while she tried something on and modeled it for him. The idea of such companionship was so bittersweet she had to shake it from her head.

At the jewelry-display counter, which doubled as the cashier's stand, the woman looked up from the stack of blouses she'd been pricing and gave Lauren a wide, magenta-lipstick smile. She looked about the same age as Lauren and wore her below-shoulder-length hair in a faux just-washed tangle.

"Can I help you find something?" she offered.

"Yes, are you Irene? Hi, I'm a friend of Sabrina Andersen's. She gave me the name of your shop and said I should drop in sometime." Lauren nodded as she glanced around. "You really do have lovely things here."

"Thank you for saying so. I own the shop, and I do all of the ordering myself." Irene beamed with pride, then added, "I haven't seen Sabrina in months. How is she? It must be terrible for her, losing Nat." She folded one arm at her waist and brought the other hand to her cheek. "How is she taking it?"

"As well as can be expected. You know how she is."

Irene frowned. "I feel sorry for her. She'll never meet another man like Nat Andersen."

"He *was* a gem. And I think they were quite happy together, don't you?"

"Yes. You know—" Irene jabbed one long, lavender fingernail at Lauren "—I was surprised when Nat proposed to her. I've known Sabrina since we were children together. I admit I thought maybe Nat was marrying her for her money or social position, and they did socialize a lot more when they were first married, but as Sabrina's condition got worse, Nat never complained." Her eyes were puzzled. "He must have understood her better than the rest of us, don't you think?"

"It would appear so. But Sabrina wasn't always so...troubled, was she?"

"No, it's gotten worse over the years, but I don't think it's had anything to do with being married. She had a pretty gloomy childhood, and then she had a kind of breakdown in college. You see, her life was fairly sheltered living in Sonoma, out in the country. Then she went off to school in Berkeley, and it was a big shock to her system. I think that's what started the real downward spiral."

"Did she meet Nat at the university?"

"Not exactly. Nat's brother, Mark, was going to Berkeley at the time, and he and Sabrina dated for a while—that's how she met Nat. I remember Mark used to come over to the sorority house and try to cheer her up. He did crazy things and almost drove Mrs. North crazy—started a fire outside in the garbage can one day! It's a wonder he didn't get expelled." Irene laughed merrily. "Then Nat started taking her out and proposed."

"I wonder what attracted him to her if she was already having problems then."

"Oh, Sabrina worshiped Nat, which probably fed his ego." Irene's eyes flicked to Bill at the front of the store and she lowered her voice. "You know how men are. Plus, I think she kind of came out of it when she met Nat. I remember she was so excited planning the wedding and starting a home. It gave her something else to think about, so she got better for a couple years. But when you've got a predisposition to melancholy, I guess it catches up with you sooner or later.''

Lauren nodded in agreement. She wanted to ask Irene about Sabrina's mother; even though the alcoholism Ada Levine had mentioned would explain the trips to emergency for cuts, which were probably sustained in drunken falls, Lauren was still hoping to find some evidence of a more violent illness in the family. ''I know Mrs. Falletti drank. Could Sabrina have inherited her psychological problems from her mother?''

Irene considered. ''She may have. I don't know what made Mrs. Falletti drink. The family kept pretty tight wraps on the fact she was an alcoholic. Being in the wine business, I guess they didn't think it a very good advertisement! They didn't do any entertaining, and still don't. But Sabrina's father is a great guy. We used to live just down the road from them, and I remember summer evenings I'd go down and try to get Sabrina to go to the movies with me or something, but she always preferred hanging out in their garage, watching her father work on those old cars of his.''

Lauren's ears perked up. ''Old cars?''

''Yes, his hobby was restoring antique automobiles. He had all kinds—Model T's, those fifties cars with the fins. He'd work on one, fix it up, then sell it.

He donated a couple to the auto museum in Reno. Sabrina used to look over his shoulder and hand him the tools. They were very close." Irene chuckled. "When she was little, Sabrina told me she wanted to grow up to be a garage mechanic."

Lauren spent a few more minutes talking with Irene, then excused herself to look around the shop. She rejoined Bill, who was standing gazing out the front window at the passersby.

She touched his arm and whispered, "Did you hear that bit about the cars?"

"Every word." He looked around. "Before we go, I'd like to get you something."

"It's not necessary for our cover. Women window-shop without buying things all the time."

"No, really, I'd like to get you a little present, honey."

The words sounded to Lauren like more playacting, but she realized with a shock he was serious when he said determinedly, "Okay, if you won't pick out something for yourself, I will."

It wouldn't do to argue with him in front of Irene, so she crossed her arms and looked about dubiously, wondering what he'd buy. She'd had presents of clothing from boyfriends before. Usually of the Frederick's of Hollywood variety! But here in this shop there wasn't a single leather mini or halter top to be seen.

Bill brushed past her and walked straight up to a wicker mannequin. "This is nice." The outfit was a baby-blue cotton pullover with a lace-trimmed Peter

Pan collar and a paisley skirt in blues and beiges. It reminded Lauren of something Princess Diana might wear. Lauren's jaw almost dropped. "This is what you want to get me?"

"Sure." Bill raised a brow. "Don't you like blue? I'm no fashion designer, but this whole outfit just looks like you, somehow. Miss!"

Irene came around the counter with a smile.

"Do you have this set in my wife's size?"

"I'm sure we do, sir."

Lauren wore a dazed look as Irene buzzed around the shop collecting the pieces. Did Bill really see her that way? As frilly and feminine and Victorian? It almost brought tears to her eyes.

Bill rubbed her back between her shoulder blades as he watched her face with confused concern. "Come on, sweetheart. It's okay. You've been working too hard. Cheer up and try it on."

As THEY EMERGED from the shop a half hour later, the sun was finally breaking through the thick layer of haze that had covered the city all morning and early afternoon. Lauren self-consciously smoothed the soft rayon fabric of her new skirt. Bill had pronounced her "as beautiful as I've ever seen you" and suggested she wear the ensemble out of the shop, then waited patiently while Irene insisted on touching up the skirt with an iron in the back room. Allowing herself to get into the spirit of things and enjoy the gift, Lauren had taken down her hair when it got mussed and purchased a blue chiffon bow to hold it back in a ponytail.

Bill placed the shopping bag with her gray suit in the trunk of the Taurus. "Before we head up to the Andersens', why don't we pay a visit to the sheriff's office?" he suggested as he came around to unlock her door. "I'd like to see if they've made any progress on the case from their end."

"Good idea. I can't wait to tell him how we sent Mark Andersen packing!"

As they merged onto the freeway, an emergency paramedic van came racing down the highway in the opposite direction, lights and siren flashing. It veered into the downtown exit; Lauren followed it with her eyes and wondered briefly where it was going. Her new sweater was warm, but a shiver shook her shoulders.

"You okay?" Bill asked.

"Yes." Lauren tried to chuckle. "You know that old expression. I just felt as though someone walked on my grave."

THEY SPENT fifteen minutes with Captain Ramsey. He had only one new piece of information for them, but it was provocative.

One of his men interviewed the maître d' at the Vineyard Restaurant. The man said Nat Andersen had dined there three days before his death with a mysterious woman.

"The headwaiter described her as tall and chesty, brown- or blond-haired, a real sexpot. Definitely not Mrs. Andersen."

Bill hid a smile with his hand as Lauren pretended not to notice.

Ramsey gave them Thomas Hinshaw's room number at Santa Rosa Memorial Hospital and permission to interview him. After that a fortuitous emergency phone call enabled them to slip away before the captain had a chance to ask them about their own investigation.

Bill put his arm around Lauren's shoulders as they walked to the car. She smiled at the sight they must have presented. She wasn't used to her investigative partners getting so familiar with her, but the pull Bill had on her was something she'd tried to fight and no longer could. All she could do now was hang on for the ride and pray it would work out between them. If it didn't, she could at least let herself enjoy it while it lasted.

"You want to talk to Hinshaw next?" Lauren asked.

"You read my mind. I just hope the butler has more to say than the chauffeur did!"

IN THE HOSPITAL LOBBY, they paused to study the building directory next to the elevator. There were several people in the elevator as the doors opened, and Lauren stepped in before she saw Allen Rogers. She barely recognized him. His usually immaculate dark hair was askew and his eyes were wide and frightened.

"Lauren, thank God you're here." He grabbed her arm as if it were a life preserver and pulled her into the elevator.

Chapter Eleven

"She's having emergency surgery right now," Allen said. "I was afraid Julie wouldn't find you...that you might not get here in time..."

The doors opened at the second floor and Allen tugged Lauren out of the elevator. Bill followed. "Allen, we haven't heard anything," Bill said. "Who's been admitted?"

"Is it my mother?" Lauren asked, thinking of her high blood pressure.

"Your mother?" Allen stared at her blankly for a moment. "No, no, it's Suzie."

"Suzie!" Lauren's hands flew to her cheeks. "God no! What happened?"

"A car accident. Another driver broadsided her."

"It's not...serious, is it?" Lauren trembled.

"I don't know." Allen ran a hand through his disheveled hair. "She's been in surgery for about an hour and we're...just waiting."

"Oh, no!" Lauren's face caved in and her shoulders crumpled. "I can't believe it. We were just with her a few hours ago. Where did it happen?"

"On Fifth Street. I was driving right behind her." Allen couldn't look at Lauren. "They had to use the jaws of life to get her out. Your car is totaled."

"It doesn't matter," Lauren said through her tears. "I'm glad it was my car. It's sturdier than that flimsy thing she drives." A sudden apprehension swept through her. "My car... No! Do they know who hit her?"

Bill stepped in. "Lauren, why don't you let me talk to Allen for a minute? Stay here by the window and I'll be right back."

Bill took the younger man a short distance down the corridor and spoke with him in a low voice. Lauren leaned sightlessly against the glass until Bill returned, alone.

"Was it Sabrina?" Lauren asked.

Bill put his hands on her forearms and gently rubbed them. "It was a small truck that hit your sister. After the crash, Allen saw a woman of about thirty with long black hair jump out of the truck and make a run for it. Apparently she got away."

"Oh, God, it *was* Sabrina! And she was after me! How could I have let Suzie use my car? What have I done?" Lauren raised both hands to the sides of her head and pressed inward.

Her expression of shock and guilt was so intense Bill was almost frightened. He grasped her wrists and pulled them down, forcing her to focus her eyes on him.

"Lauren, this wasn't your fault. *You* didn't run into Suzie. You had no way of knowing this would happen."

"I had someone surveilling Sabrina until last night, when I ran out of money. I could have tried to hire someone else. I could have borrowed the money, but I didn't. . . ."

Lauren began to sob as Bill tried to hold her shoulders and calm her. She fought him off, swinging her arms wide and fending off his hands. "I've got to call the police. Let me go!" she cried. "I've got to tell them to arrest Sabrina."

"Lauren. Lauren!" He caught hold of her flailing arms. "I'll call them. Calm down! I'll tell them about you and Nat Andersen and have them take Sabrina in for questioning."

Lauren stopped struggling and at last allowed Bill to fold her in his arms. She continued crying as he held her head against his chest.

"I feel like it's my fault, Bill," she said. "*I* should have been the one in that car."

"I know, I know," he said soothingly, then added, though he was by no means sure of it, "It's going to be all right."

LAUREN LOOKED UP as a man clothed in surgical green strode into the waiting area. Allen had already seen him and was on his feet.

"Mr. Rogers, is it? I'm Dr. Wojcik." He extended his hand.

"This is Suzie's mother, Margaret Pierce," Allen said, then introduced Lauren and Bill.

"Why don't we all sit down for a moment?" the doctor said.

Bill frowned as they arranged themselves on the cobalt blue upholstered furniture.

"Will Suzie be okay?" Allen asked.

"I'm very pleased with how the surgery went. We removed Susan's spleen—it was ruptured—and we've stopped the abdominal bleeding."

"Doctor, what exactly is the spleen?" Mrs. Pierce asked. "Is it something she can live without, like an appendix?"

"Yes," Wojcik replied. "The spleen isn't a vital organ. I don't think you need to worry on that score. However—" his brow knit "—following the surgery, I had a CAT scan done of Susan's head, and there is some swelling of the soft tissues, what we call a cerebral edema. There are no lesions or bleeding in the brain, but she's still unconscious, and it's very important that the swelling go down."

Dr. Wojcik cleared his throat and addressed Mrs. Pierce. "You should know that your daughter's still in critical condition. We've got an ICP line going into the skull so we can monitor the brain pressure, and she's on a respirator. We're going to keep a close watch on her, but we've done all we can for her at this point. It's up to her now."

Bill circled Lauren's shaking shoulders with his arm. Dr. Wojcik sat silently for some moments as Allen stared numbly at the carpet and Mrs. Pierce covered her eyes and wept softly.

Finally the doctor spoke again. "I'm hoping she'll regain consciousness within the next forty-eight hours. Either way, as soon as her condition changes, I'll let you see her. Has the rest of her family been notified?"

Allen roused himself. "We're all here, except for Suzie's aunt, who lives up in Oregon."

Bill watched as Wojcik laid his hand on Allen's knee. "Perhaps you should try to call her." His calmness was so forced it was grim.

THEY HAD THE TWO-ROOM, windowless waiting area all to themselves. Lauren and Bill sat together, Mrs. Pierce and Allen across from them. A small television mounted on a pedestal squawked incessantly. No one talked.

As evening wore into night, there was little news of Suzie's condition. The nurses would have kept them informed, but Allen, unable to relax, made periodic trips to the nurse's station to check on her. By eleven there was still no change.

Lauren got up and mumbled something about getting a drink from the water fountain, and Bill followed her. Though she'd stopped crying, he could tell that pain and guilt were eating at her, and he longed to do something to ease her distress.

The hospital was fairly quiet at this late hour, and the hall was deserted. Lauren bent over the fountain and took a drink. When she straightened, Bill was leaning against the wall beside her. Unable to keep her tortured thoughts to herself any longer, she said, "I can't believe this has happened now, not when Suzie was so happy, when everything was coming together in her life and she was getting married."

He reached out for her and she sagged against him.

"I have a terrible confession to make," she said, pressing her temple into the rough tweed of his jacket. "I...I was jealous of Suzie. Of her and Allen. Which makes me feel even more as though I brought this on—"

"Shh, shh, I understand," Bill said. "What you felt was perfectly natural. She's younger than you, and I can't believe you actually took any of your envy out on her."

"No, of course not. I was happy for her, too, but just the same..."

"It doesn't matter now, Lauren. Suzie knows how much you love her. Let it go."

As she leaned on him, Bill relished the feeling of his arms around her slim shoulders and her breasts softly nestled against his shirt. It was like the most wonderful dream he'd ever had, coming true in the midst of the most terrible nightmare.

Her hair was mussed, golden wisps escaping her ponytail and trailing past her delicate, shell-like ears. Even with her aqua eyes turned red and puffy he still found her lovely, the most beautiful woman he'd ever known. And it wasn't just her looks that attracted him like a magnet—it was her goodness, her caring for those around her, her strength. But she was also vulnerable, and right now she needed him.

He wanted to kiss her, to comfort and reassure her with his lips. But the very fragility that prompted his impulse made him hold back. She might not understand, might feel it unseemly to forget her troubles in a kiss when her sister's life hung in the balance. Though Lauren's stubbornness and his desire for her had driven him to distraction more than once, he'd never wanted to hurt her, and he wouldn't risk it now. For the moment, perhaps all he could do was hold her and thank God they'd cleared up their misunderstandings when they had.

They stood together quietly for several minutes. Then Lauren slowly pulled away and reached into the pocket of her new skirt for a tissue. "Thank you," she said, whisking away her tears. "You're a good comforter." She smiled and stood on tiptoe to kiss his cheek, then bowed her head as she softly blew her nose.

"I think we'd better get back to my mother and Allen," she said stoically. "It's hardest on my mother. She and Suzie have always been the closest."

Bill thought of how Margaret Pierce had sat across the room from Lauren all night, holding Allen's hand for support. Bill didn't know what the story was about Margaret's relationship with Lauren, but it was clear the older woman felt closer to her future son-in-law than her own daughter.

"Lauren—" Bill took her hand in both of his "—I know how much Suzie means to *you*, not just to your mother. Anytime you need someone to lean on, I'll be here."

"Come on," Lauren said, giving him a wan little smile as she dabbed at a fresh tear. "If you keep saying things like that, I'll never stop crying."

Bill put his arm around her shoulders and they walked back to the waiting room.

IT WAS A LONG NIGHT. Bill finally turned off the television at the conclusion of an old black-and-white movie. Allen looked up, startled by the sound of the TV clicking off, and Bill wondered if the poor man had even realized it was on.

It suddenly came home to Bill how easily it could have been him sitting there, half out of his mind with worry, while Lauren lay in intensive care. The thought made his stomach turn. He glanced at Lauren, who sat next to him with her fingers laced through his. Reassured, he let his thoughts drift back to the accident.

Had the crash been intentional or an accident? Was it really Sabrina who'd rammed the stolen pickup into Suzie? The description fit, but a lot of young men wore their hair long again these days. Could it have been some kid out for a joyride, too spaced out on drugs to notice the silver Toyota as he peeled out of the parking lot?

Bill had to consider every possibility. He looked at the accident from several angles, then rejected the theories. No. It had to have been Sabrina. It was too much of a coincidence. Unless . . .

Lauren's head slowly drifted to his chest as she dozed, but Bill stayed awake, his mind going over and over the conflicting facts as he tried to piece them together.

LAUREN GAVE A START, suddenly wide-awake, around four in the morning. She looked about. Her mother's head was against Allen's shoulder while Allen's head rested on hers. Bill's eyes were closed and his breathing was steady and slow; he'd finally dropped off, too. But Lauren was afraid to go back to sleep. She'd heard that most people die in the hours just before dawn, and the thought chilled her. She wrapped her arm around Bill's and prayed, asking God to help Suzie, to make the swelling in her skull go down and to give her strength while she fought through the last hours of the night.

It seemed like an eternity before the sky started to grow light outside.

The nurse came in a little before seven, and Lauren gently nudged her mother and Allen to rouse them. As she did so, Bill awoke, then rubbed his neck and grimaced.

"Susan is doing better," the nurse said. "She's still not conscious, but the swelling has subsided."

"Is she really better?" Allen asked, his bleary eyes suddenly coming alert.

"Yes. Her condition has been upgraded from critical to serious. The doctor is with her now, but you can see her in a few minutes when he's finished."

"Thank God!" Allen said as Lauren gave a little cry of joy and bounced up to hug her mother's shoulders.

Dr. Wojcik was just leaving Suzie's room as the nurse showed them down the hall. "She's not out of the woods yet," he warned them, "but she's doing much better." The doctor allowed himself a momentary smile before his face grew serious again.

"She's still unconscious and will be for at least another eighteen hours. I didn't go into it last night, because I knew you had enough on your minds, but she has a facial fracture that will require some reconstructive surgery in three to ten days. Injuries of this type aren't pretty, but they often look worse than they actually are. I've got another patient to see, but I'll be back to check on her in a few hours."

Lauren and her mother entered the room first, the men close behind. Lauren almost gasped when she saw her sister. Suzie's face was swathed in bandages so that only her swollen, purplish eyelids were visible. A wide plastic tube led from her mouth to a bellowslike respirator, and a tube stretched from her partially shaven scalp to a small monitor. Two IVs, one dripping blood, another a clear liquid, were inserted in her left arm, which was taped to the bed rail.

"My God!" Mrs. Pierce cried, grabbing Lauren's arm and stumbling toward the bed. "All these machines! It's terrible."

"Well, better the machines than not," Lauren said lightly, trying to think positively. "Thank goodness Suzie was born in the twentieth century."

"If she'd been born in another century, she wouldn't have been nearly killed by an automobile!" her mother snapped, then immediately looked sorry. She started to say something, then changed her mind and just squeezed Lauren's arm before leaning over the bed to speak softly to her younger daughter. Bill frowned at the exchange.

There wasn't much for them to do. The nurse kept a respectful watch as Mrs. Pierce, Lauren and then Allen took turns briefly holding Suzie's free hand. Her fingers were warm, Lauren noted with some comfort; it seemed a good sign.

As Allen bent over his fiancée to whisper something, Lauren forced herself to take a second look at the monitors ringing the bed and to study the rhythmic rise and fall of Suzie's chest. Lauren wasn't a doctor, but to her layman's eye Suzie appeared stable, and she sensed that Dr. Wojcik, despite all his disclaimers, had been genuinely pleased with his patient's condition. She wished Suzie would wake up, but she told herself it was probably better for her sister that she remain unconscious for a while. Once she was awake, there would be the pain and psychological trauma for her to deal with, and that would only sap her strength.

As they emerged from the hospital room, Allen escorted Mrs. Pierce, who was looking hopeful despite the initial shock. It seemed safe for Lauren to leave the hospital for a few hours, so she asked Bill if he'd drive her home. She wanted to change and maybe take a nap.

As soon as she and Bill were out of earshot of the others, Lauren began to giggle. By the time they'd descended the stairs and emerged from the lobby into the parking lot, she was almost doubled over.

"You're sure you're okay?" Bill teased. "You haven't gone around the bend or something?"

"No, no." Lauren tried to catch her breath. "It's just that I always laugh when I'm afraid. When Suzie and I were kids, she almost sliced the tip of her finger off with a paring knife and it bled something awful. Our mother came running and wrapped it up in a towel. As soon as I was sure Suzie was going to be okay, I started laughing hysterically." Lauren coughed as she wiped her eyes. "Lord, I am so relieved! Suzie means the world to me. I just hope she won't be permanently disfigured."

Bill put his arm around her and her hand gratefully circled his waist as they walked to the car.

"It's too early to worry about that now," he said. "But even if she's left with a scar or two, no one is going to notice. Allen clearly loves her so much it won't make a bit of difference to him, and Suzie doesn't strike me as the kind of girl who's vain about her appearance."

"Yes." A lump formed in Lauren's throat. "She's a special kid, and a real trooper. I never realized how tough she is. I always thought *I* was the strong one." Lauren shook her head in wonder.

Bill opened the car door for her. She watched as he circled the car and slid behind the wheel. For such a big man he was amazingly light on his feet, moving with that unconscious self-assurance that had become so familiar to her. Being with him all the time felt natural now. It would seem strange to say goodbye to him when he dropped her off.

As they drove, she said, "It was wonderful of you to stay all night with us, when you barely know Suzie."

"I'm glad she's going to recover." He reached out and curled her hand in his.

"I don't know how I would have gotten through last night without you," she said softly.

She wasn't surprised when he didn't say anything, just kept his eyes on the road. He wouldn't expect thanks, for the same reason she wouldn't have expected thanks if she'd spent the night by *his* side: they were deeply drawn to one another.

Lauren leaned back in the car seat, realizing that a cocoon of intimacy had grown around them in the long, dark hours of the night, binding them like a thousand fine yet steel-strong threads. Bill had proved he cared about her on much more than a physical level, and that assurance freed her, excited her, filled her with anticipation for where this relationship might lead.

Ever since they'd walked into the hospital and learned about Suzie, there had hardly been a moment when he wasn't holding her hand, stroking her hair to soothe her, reassuringly holding her shoulders. Now, as they drove in silence through the streets of a new day, she sensed that comforting, protective energy begin to subtly change and reform itself.

She felt it in the possessive pressure of his fingers, registered it in the quickened beat of her pulse, smelled it in the masculine scent of his sweat.

The air in the car grew thicker, as though fate, like some great buildup of electricity, was charging the atmosphere. Lightning was coming.

Bill parked the car in front of her place. A shiver went through her as he took her hand and led her up the walk. She fumbled with the key, his eyes on her as she let them in, shut the door and leaned against the foyer wall. It was very quiet in the condo. Like stepping from the outer world into some darkened, secret cave. They were alone.

He braced his hands on the wall over her head, trapping her as they drank in one another's eyes. "I should let you get some rest," he said.

Something tingled in Lauren's stomach. She could feel the primal aura of his body enfolding her; the hunter, weakening and dissolving any desire for resistance, making it impossible for her to flee.

Bill massaged her shoulders with his heated hands, ran his palms up her neck, then stroked her jawline with the pads of his thumbs up to the sensitive skin behind her ears. Lauren closed her eyes, wanting to purr like a cat.

"Will you be okay here alone?" he asked. "They've probably picked up Sabrina by now. I can call and ask Ramsey."

But he didn't move a hair. She knew that he was teasing her. That he had no intention of leaving. But she was neither angry nor afraid. After last night, she no longer doubted his feelings for her. She knew he would stop if she asked him to.

"I'm all right," she said boldly, "but I don't want to be alone."

He smiled sardonically, one brow arched. "You know, you are a pretty remarkable lady, Ms. Pierce. My life hasn't been the same since I met you. Not a day has passed that I haven't lived for your soft smile and to hear you say my name—" his voice grew husky "—or a night I haven't dreamed of making love to you. I hold you personally responsible for that."

"Good," Lauren said, sucking in her lip and gently pounding her fist into his shirt over his heart. "I wouldn't want it any other way."

She tilted her chin, and his lips were there to meet hers. Her arms glided up, curling behind his neck.

Tenderly, almost desperately, he kissed her mouth, then her cheeks and her eyelids, her forehead. It was as though he wanted to show his desire not only for her body but for her mind and soul, as well. In the ardor of his kiss she felt his love for her, his pride in her, his need for her. She clung to him, wanting to give him everything.

His pace slowed as his mouth melded with hers again. The kiss deepened and became sensual, a kind of exotic music that was rich and mysterious and totally captivating. Lauren lost track of all else as her senses ignited.

His hands caressed her sides, running from under her arms to her waist and back again. They burned a path under her sweater and around her middle. As his fingers splayed over the small of her back, pressing her in to himself, they threatened to scorch her flimsy blouse. She could feel him through the wool of his trousers, big, hard, aching for her.

She mouthed his rough cheek, running her tongue over the short jagged scar, pressed her moist lips to his ear and whispered, "Bill, take me to bed."

He slowly pulled back, his breathing jagged as he pushed himself to arm's length and studied her face. "That's what I want, sweetheart, but I want you to be sure."

Lauren pushed her fingertips deep into the hair at the back of his neck and felt a shiver shake his broad shoulders. She sighed and cocked her head to one side, her swollen lower lip pouty. "Really, Donelan, why must you always argue with me?"

With one swift movement Bill caught her up under the knees and carried her back to the bedroom.

Chapter Twelve

Bill set Lauren down on the cream satin comforter of her queen-size bed. Rays of light slanted through the venetian blind at the window, making a pattern on the wall that reminded him of an old Bogart-Bacall movie.

"Do you mind the light?" he asked. "I can close the blind more."

Lauren shook her head. She wanted no barriers between them on this, their first time, even one as amorphous as the dark.

As Bill began to undress, she lay on the bed and watched, luxuriating in a delicious sense of anticipation. Her past experiences, when she'd been a college girl, seemed distant now. Gone were the uncertainty and consequent disappointment she'd struggled with then. She felt no shame or self-consciousness about her body. Only a sense of rightness she was sure she could feel with no other man.

Bill unzipped his trousers and stepped out of them. Excitement swirled in her stomach as he hiked down his shorts and tossed them aside.

Lauren's eyes widened and a tiny gasp escaped her lips. Bill Donelan stood before her naked, magnificent. He reminded her of Michelangelo's David, grown into full manhood.

He knelt on one knee next to the bed. "Do you know you look just like the cat who ate the cream?" he asked.

Now she did blush. "You put on quite a show, sir. I suppose if I was more maidenly, I'd be hiding under the sheets."

"I'm glad you're not." He took her hand. "You never need to be afraid with me."

"I'm definitely not that," she said, her lips curving upward. She let her fingers glide over the hair above one of his nipples, along his shoulder and around the massive, curved muscle of his biceps. "I'm not afraid, though I do feel a little weak in the legs," she admitted.

"I'll help you," he said, pulling her gently to her feet. He stayed her hands as they reached for her hair. "May I?"

He released her ponytail from the bow, then lightly massaged her hairline. She closed her eyes as he ran his fingers along her scalp from hairline to nape.

"Your hair is beautiful, like every inch of you," he said, arranging the chestnut tresses behind her shoulders. He kissed her on the mouth as he ran his hands under her sweater, then whispered, "Raise your arms."

Obediently she held them up so he could pull the garment over her head; then she stepped out of her new skirt and turned, lifting her hair so he could unfasten the row of buttons on the back of her blouse. He slid the blouse forward over her shoulders, and it slithered in a puddle at their feet.

She could feel his breath on her neck, hear his deep breathing behind her as his hands came over her collarbone, down the silky front of her teddy. Her nipples formed into stiff points as his hands passed over them, then down and under the camisole and up, enveloping her breasts. He slowly caressed them as he nibbled the lobe of her ear, the side of her neck. Lauren arched her back and moaned. She wriggled her bottom against him, pushing his member into her back. She regretted the layers of fabric that still covered her throbbing loins, wishing she was naked and that he might enter her right now.

"We're almost there, darling," he whispered, releasing her so she could remove her slip, then her stockings.

Still behind her, his hands briefly cupped the firm crescents of her buttocks and she heard him sigh in admiration. Then he kissed her shoulder as his arms came around her. His right hand played beneath her teddy, making love again to her breasts. His other hand trailed down over her ribs, her stomach, kneading with a circular motion the soft skin of her belly.

When her knees began to sag, he splayed his fingers across her abdomen and held her up as he helped her slip the camisole over her head.

With great tenderness he lowered her to the bed, allowing his eyes to feast for a moment on the perfect round swells of her breasts. Her closed eyes and pouting lips inflamed his own desire, bringing him perilously close to the edge. To distract himself, he reached for his wallet on the nightstand and took out the condom he had stored there. Lauren opened her eyes briefly, but he was glad when she didn't offer to help him; if she touched him again he might lose his tenuous control, and he didn't want to disappoint her.

He covered her mouth with his as once more his hand traced down her body, going all the way this time to explore the soft curls between her legs. He felt, as well as heard, her sharp intake of breath as his fingers parted her downy lips. He sought and found the entrance to her secret place, pushed his index finger inside where it was hot and sticky moist. With his thumb he located her nub of pleasure, then began working his fingers in slow, tight circles, bringing her alive.

Lauren disengaged her mouth from his and moaned, curling her knees up around his hand. When her body began to convulse, he parted her knees and eased himself between her legs.

Bill schooled himself to go slowly, to not hurt her. She was tight, and he could tell it had been a long time since she'd been with anyone, perhaps even as long as he himself had waited.

Lauren felt her muscles pull him into herself, upward, toward her heart. Her soul expanded even as his body filled her. It was a delirious feeling of being completely loved, completely accepted, completely whole. In turn, she felt herself reaching out, enfolding Bill, making him forever a part of her.

Bill raised himself up slightly and slowly began to move back and forth inside her. His hand remained cupped over her, his finger stroking, stroking, stroking in time with his thrusts.

Each movement brought her exquisite pleasure and seemed to take him deeper inside her. She wound her legs around his waist, moving with him. She clung to him for support as first ripples, then waves of ecstasy passed through her. When she began to think she could endure such exquisite torture no longer, she felt Bill begin to shake. He hoarsely, almost fearfully, called out her name as she herself cried out and they rode the last, explosive wave together.

THEY LAY ENTWINED for some time, her hot cheek resting on the sweaty pillow of his chest; he was so tall the top of her head only came to his chin. He stroked her arm as she listened to the gradually slowing beat of his heart.

When he kissed her and rose to go into the bathroom, Lauren decided to wait until he turned on the shower, then join him. She lay on her back on top of the comforter, feeling strangely empty now that he was no longer inside her. It reminded her of something she'd once heard, that a woman with child felt as though she constantly carried her man inside her. She rubbed her hand over her belly, wondering what it would be like to feel Bill's comforting fullness there for nine months, to carry the natural fruit of their lovemaking.

She looked up to find Bill watching her silently from the doorway, still nude except for a towel slung around his neck.

"You're so beautiful," he said. He sat down beside her and picked up her hand, kissing her curled fingers. "I can't find the words to tell you how I feel, Lauren. I wish I could."

As her gaze dropped, she saw he wanted her again and was physically ready to act on the impulse.

She laughed in surprise and rekindled anticipation.

For a moment she thought she'd hurt his feelings, because his brow furrowed.

"I try to be romantic, and you get the giggles."

"I'm sorry, darling," she said, "honestly. I know I'm acting silly, but I suddenly feel so...so light-hearted and happy."

He grinned. "I hope I had something to do with that, so I won't complain. And just to prove I'm no spoilsport..."

Lauren let out a screech as he grabbed her and they rolled across the bed together.

Sometime later, as they lay exhausted, Lauren growled into her lover's ear, "You, sir, are a lady-killer."

"If you ask me, sweetheart, it was a case of mutual murder."

THEY SHOWERED, then slept naked in each other's arms until noon. Lauren got up first and, clad in her pink terry robe, went out to the kitchen to fix them some breakfast.

Bill appeared in his slacks and T-shirt as she was frying eggs. He clamped his arms around her, nuzzling her already wild hair and threatening to make her burn the eggs.

"Why don't you wait in the living room?" she said, laughing and attempting to dislodge him. "Food'll be ready in just a few minutes. Go on, shoo."

He kissed the top of her head, then took himself out to the living room and flopped into an easy chair.

He felt rested, content and wonderfully relaxed. Besides having just spent the most fulfilling morning of his life, he found the atmosphere in this house inviting, comforting. Looking about, he was struck by how functional his own place was compared to this. He'd lived in the same apartment in L.A. for ten years, and yet he hadn't felt a twinge of sentiment when he moved out six weeks ago. His digs had always been simply a place to sleep and shave, to play his old movies on the stereo VCR, to cook a TV dinner in the microwave.

He was a trained observer, and he'd noticed all the little touches Lauren gave this place. The kitchen cupboards neatly lined with shelf paper, the basket of rolled-up hand towels in the guest bath, the hummingbird feeder on the back patio. There was even a pine needle sticking out of the carpet over there in the corner, marking where a Christmas tree had undoubtedly stood the month before. All these things told him clearly that Lauren's condominium was more than a place to crash. It was a home.

He wondered how his own things would look here. There was plenty of empty space against that wall for one of his vintage movie posters; it would look fine with her modern cream-on-white furniture, and she could choose which one. His stereo was better quality, so they could keep his, and it would fit perfectly in her combination entertainment center and bookcase, though if he knew Lauren, she'd probably want to load its shelves with their wedding pictures—

"Breakfast is ready!" Lauren called.

For a moment he imagined he heard their child racing down the hall yelling, "Is it pancakes, Mommy?"

Bill shook his head, blinked and laughed.

Lauren stood at the table in her robe, hands on hips. "You okay, Donelan?"

"Yes, just daydreaming."

Lauren's brow wrinkled. "What about? No, don't tell me, Mr. Wolf. I can guess." She grinned.

Bill raised himself out of the chair. "No, it wasn't that, though that *would* be very nice, too."

"So what is it?" She opened her arms automatically as he moved up to her.

He gave her a bear hug and kissed her on the forehead. "Maybe one day I'll tell you. Man, this looks good. Let's eat."

AN HOUR LATER they headed back to Santa Rosa Memorial Hospital, stopping on the way at Bill's apartment so he could shave and change clothes. They checked in on Suzie first, then took the elevator to the third floor and over to the north wing to interview the Andersen butler, Thomas Hinshaw.

The door was open; Bill rapped lightly on it with his knuckles as he stuck his head inside.

The bed nearest the door was empty, but a man was sitting in the other one, propped up on his pillows watching television.

"May we come in?" Lauren called.

"Who's that?" Hinshaw clicked the mute switch on the TV's remote control and squinted at them from behind horn-rimmed glasses. He looked to be in his midfifties, with brown hair that was carefully combed over his balding head.

"Who are you?" he demanded. "Not more reporters? I thought you'd all left last night."

The two P.I.'s walked up to the bed. "No, Mr. Hinshaw," Bill said, "we're private investigators, working with the sheriff's department. My name is Bill Donelan and this is Lauren Pierce."

"Got any ID?"

Lauren pulled her case from her purse and held it out to him. He carefully scrutinized it, then did the same with Bill's.

Hinshaw pushed Bill's hand away. "Well, that's all right then." With a jab of the remote he turned off the TV. "Has something new come up?"

Lauren was tempted to get his reaction to Sabrina's being arrested, but she knew it wasn't her place to tell him. "I'm afraid if you want to know about the case, you'll have to ask one of the sheriff's deputies." Lauren glanced down at the bedclothes. There was no evidence to suggest what Hinshaw's injuries were, but nonetheless, she said, "It looks like you had a pretty harrowing time in that crash."

"Oh, it was awful, awful!" the butler exclaimed with relish. "Got an unstable pelvic fracture and a femur fracture." Now that they'd properly identified themselves, he seemed to have no compunction about telling them all about it. He proceeded to describe, in lurid detail, just how he'd thrown himself from the car and when and how each of his injuries had occurred. Bill stood beside Lauren as she sat in a chair at the foot of the bed and they both pretended to be fascinated by the monologue.

After about ten minutes, Hinshaw began to wind down. "The doctor tells me I'll be in here for some time more, but that doesn't matter—the Andersens are paying for it."

Seeing his chance, Bill broke in. "We're glad to see you're feeling so much better. Now, if you don't mind, we need to ask you some questions about the night of the accident. The phone call that came for Mr. Andersen, supposedly from the plant—are you sure it was a woman's voice?"

"Yes. It was a bit husky, rather like someone trying to change her voice so you wouldn't recognize it, but it was a woman. I'm sure of that."

"During the ride down the mountain," Lauren said, "did Mr. Andersen say anything when he realized the car was starting to go out of control?"

"Nothing but a few choice swear words." Hinshaw grunted. "He was too busy for anything else!"

"Do you remember exactly what he said?" Lauren persisted.

The butler hesitated. "He was struggling to control the car, but that heavy limousine picked up speed incredibly fast." For the first time, Hinshaw paled a bit at the memory. "He was trying to run us onto the uphill bank, to slow us down, but we were in danger of overturning. The last time he tried it, the car ricocheted off the bank and headed for the cliff. Somewhere along the way, I'm not sure where, he said, 'Son of a bitch.' He said it quickly, several times—his teeth must have been clenched because it sounded funny—hissy, like a snake. I was bracing myself and looking out the front, so I didn't see his face as he spoke."

"Are you sure he said, 'Son of a bitch'?" Bill asked. "Was that all he said?"

Hinshaw scratched his cheek and was thoughtful a moment. "I'm sure I heard the word 'bitch'—that's quite clear in my mind. But he could have said, 'It's a bitch.' No, that doesn't sound right—it was more of an *s* sound right at the beginning of the first word."

Lauren said, "Could it have been, 'She's a bitch'?"

"Well, that wouldn't make any sense. Oh, I see what you mean—he was swearing at the car, maybe. Yes, that's quite possible. But what difference does it really make? 'Son of a bitch,' or, 'She's a bitch,' the poor man still went over the side, God have mercy."

Lauren smiled with satisfaction, and she couldn't help throwing a little triumphant smirk at Bill. She was tempted to tell the man in the bed that it did make a difference, a very big difference, what Nat Andersen's last words had been, but she resisted the temptation. Better to let the sheriff's men ask him about it again later, when it might have come even clearer to him. She didn't want to be accused of coaching a witness who could put Sabrina away!

From the hallway, a female voice said, "I see you're back, Officer. Can I get you a chair?"

"Excuse me," Bill told Lauren and Hinshaw, and went to the door. A young police officer in a black parka stood just outside the door, sipping coffee from a paper cup. He jerked when he saw Bill, and the coffee nearly burned his hand.

"Sorry if I startled you," Bill said.

"That's okay, I just left for a minute.... I mean...I thought the, ah, gentleman, was alone." The cop's eyes narrowed. "Are you a relative, sir?"

"No, my name's Donelan. I've been working with Captain Ramsey of the sheriff's department on the Andersen case. I own a private detective agency in town."

"Oh, I see." The policeman smiled in relief.

"I didn't know they were posting a guard on Mr. Hinshaw," Bill said.

"Oh, yeah. Didn't you hear about Sabrina Andersen?"

Lauren stepped up beside Bill as he said, "They've arrested her, haven't they?"

"No. A warrant went out for her last evening, but she's disappeared. The deputies went up to the house after dinnertime, and the maid said she'd gone out shopping at the Santa Rosa Mall. When the deputies got down there they found her limousine and driver, and the guy was in a terrible state. He said he'd driven her down there for an hour's shopping and she never came out. The deputies and some of our guys from Santa Rosa PD combed the mall, but they couldn't find her."

"Were the deputies able to ascertain her movements of yesterday afternoon?" Bill asked.

"I think the housekeeper told them she'd been in bed with a headache all day and didn't get up till early evening, but she's supposed to have run down some woman in Santa Rosa in a stolen truck yesterday afternoon."

"Yes, we know about that." Lauren thought of explaining she was the victim's sister, but decided to skip it.

"You all through here?" Bill asked her.

"Yes, if you are."

Bill smiled at the young cop. "Don't let yourself get bored sitting out here all day."

"Hey, it's better than being on the street." He gave them a nod as they left.

With Sabrina on the loose, Bill suggested it was time Lauren start carrying her gun, so they drove to the office for it. As they emerged from the elevator, Lauren said, "That's odd. My office door is open."

"I thought you called Julie last night and told her to take today off," Bill said in a low voice.

"I did."

Bill held out his left arm to keep her back and, reaching under his jacket, pulled out his automatic.

Chapter Thirteen

He held Lauren back with his left hand while he stealthily approached the office door and looked in. A second later he turned and motioned her forward.

"Don't look so relieved," he said. "You've had a visitor."

As she came up beside him, she saw the frosted glass on the door had been shattered. Julie was inside, standing there in her coat, looking bewildered. Then Lauren saw the mess.

The office looked as though a cyclone had passed through it—only the walls were still standing. Everywhere there were papers, spread out on the floor like a wild carpet and hanging off the overturned chairs and tables.

"Oh, Lauren!" Julie said. "I decided to come in and pick up some things. I just walked in a minute ago, and found everything like this!"

Bill still had his gun out. He made a sweep of Lauren's office and the file room, then holstered the weapon and told them it was clear.

Lauren stepped as lightly as she could on the papers. When they saw her office, she and Julie let out gasps of dismay.

Not only were there papers everywhere, but the venetian blind hung askew, her vinyl executive chair had been slashed with a knife so that the stuffing protruded, her computer was dashed to the floor, and Lauren's diplomas, license and framed photos were pulled off the walls and smashed facedown.

Lauren stepped into the room, trying to push back with her toe the files that had been thrown from gaping cabinets.

"Bloody hell. Who did this?" Julie asked, her voice shaking. Then Lauren heard her groan, and she turned. Julie was staring at the wall behind them. Scrawled with bright red lipstick in letters two feet high was the word "Harlot."

"I would say someone isn't pleased with me," Lauren quipped, and frowned grimly.

"This is disgusting, absolutely disgusting," Julie declared.

Lauren didn't feel as casual about the devastation as she sounded, but she wasn't about to be cowed, either. She started to ask Bill to call the police, then decided, considering Julie's shaken state, to give her something to do. "Julie, call the police department right away and have them come up here—they've got to go over everything before we can start cleaning up. I'll call Ed Ramsey and tell him where Sabrina Andersen was last night. And don't touch anything. You can use a handkerchief or paper towel to hold the phone."

"Yes, of course." Julie looked relieved to have a course of action, and she made her way gingerly back to her desk.

"What's missing?" Bill asked as Lauren rummaged through her office.

She slammed her desk drawer shut. "My revolver, for starters." She gently lifted by the edges the papers surrounding the area where her computer had sat. "My backup diskettes box seems to be gone. I had the Andersen file out on my desk yesterday morning. I wouldn't be surprised if it's gone now, too."

The second phone line rang. Bill whipped out his handkerchief before Lauren could react and picked up the receiver.

A male voice said, "Hello. Is Miss Pierce there?"

Making a quick decision, Bill said, "No, I'm sorry. She stepped out to run an errand. May I take a message?"

"Who is this?"

"My name's Donelan. I'm an associate of hers. You can leave the message with me."

"Very well. Tell her I called. I'm the former plant manager at the River Bend Lumber Mill up here in Healdsburg, the one owned by the Andersen family that they've decided to close down. I've got some information to give Miss Pierce about Mrs. Sabrina Andersen."

"When can you come in and see us?"

"I can't come there, and I won't talk to anyone except Miss Pierce. Tell her if she wants to speak to me, I'll be here at the mill for another hour. My office is a hundred yards due east of the front gate. Tell her to come alone, or I won't speak to her."

"I understand," Bill said. "Thank you for calling."

"Who was that?" Lauren asked as Bill hung up, his jaw working in thought.

"The plant manager at River Bend Lumber. He says the Andersens are shutting down the operation, so he's willing to give us some information about Sabrina." Bill neglected to mention that the man had said he'd only talk to Lauren.

For a moment Lauren was suspicious, but Bill looked so at ease she relaxed. "That's wonderful! Where are we meeting him?"

"At the mill in Healdsburg, but I'll have to go alone because he says he can't wait."

When she started to object, he said, "Someone's got to stay here and tell Ramsey that Sabrina hit this place last night. The police will be here any minute, so just stay put and you'll be safe. I'll call you in about an hour."

Lauren nodded. What he said made sense, but there was a strange feeling in the bottom of her stomach as she kissed him goodbye.

When she called Captain Ramsey, she was told he was in a meeting and couldn't be disturbed. The secretary was so adamant about not interrupting him that Lauren figured he must either be in a personnel hearing or meeting with the sheriff himself. However, his secretary agreed to have him call Lauren as soon as he got out. Lauren briefly considered asking to speak to one of the two lieutenants who was working the case, but decided against it since she'd had no prior contact with either of them.

That done, she righted the reception-area chairs and sat down with Julie to wait for the Santa Rosa Police to arrive and dust the office for prints.

BILL PEERED out the window of the Taurus at the cloudy afternoon sky. It had been sunny earlier when he and Lauren had left her condominium, but now the sun was completely obliterated by low, sooty clouds.

He was heading south down Old Redwood Highway into the country. Rutted, fallow fields and leafless apple orchards stretched solemnly from the road to the banks of the Russian River, half a mile to the west. Up ahead, the main gate of River Bend Lumber stood open.

He pulled in through the gate in the chain-link fence and slowed the car. The caller had told the truth when he said the plant was being abandoned. Although the buildings were in good shape, there was zero activity: no movement, no sign of human beings, no noise.

Ahead, through a canyon of buildings, a solitary white sedan was parked in front of a clapboard shack. Bill removed the automatic from his pocket, released the safety and held it out of sight in his lap as he slowly pulled forward.

He scanned the base of the conical furnace to his left and the two-story, windowless factory building to his right as he drove between them and parked next to the sedan.

There was a darker, square patch of paint on the shack where a sign had probably once hung, but someone had removed it, and there were no lights on inside. He wasn't surprised when he tried the door and found it locked.

He'd realized immediately that the call to Lauren's office was probably bogus, a trap. He wouldn't have insisted on coming alone otherwise. But he was determined to stop the woman who was stalking Lauren, and he knew the best way to do that would be to come alone to the mill, to take the woman quickly and by surprise before she had time to run to ground again. If he'd brought the police with him she would doubtless have been spooked, and if she slipped away there was no telling when or where she might strike at Lauren again.

There was a rush of air and something slapped hard at the sleeve of Bill's jacket. Automatically he dived around the corner of the shack and waited for the next shot. When none came, he darted a look around the building.

He spotted her. She was on the roof of the factory building. Though she was prone with a hunting rifle in her hands, there was no mistaking the long, lank, dark hair.

He was about to change his position, try to get around and up behind her on the roof, when a bullet exploded into the corner of the building. A loose board ripped off, catching him in the temple and slamming him backward onto the ground.

When he opened his eyes, blood was seeping into the right one and the left was strangely dark and unfocused. With horror, he realized he'd been knocked unconscious and was close to passing out again. As he struggled to sit up, he cursed the luck that had suddenly turned on him. If he stayed here another moment, the shooter would surely descend on him and he'd be dead.

Fighting to keep his mind clear, he remembered there was a corrugated metal building behind him with a wide second-story balcony. If the woman was still on the factory roof, the overhang would shield him from her fire. If he could just make it those few yards!

Unsteadily he rose to his feet and stumbled to the building. A shot rang out. Damn! She'd seen him. He pressed his handkerchief to his bleeding temple as he felt his way along under the balcony, came to a door that was slightly ajar and looked in. The interior of the building was filled with some kind of machinery.

The pain in his head was fierce and his vision seemed to be getting narrower by the second. He took deep breaths, fought for consciousness. He still had his gun, but it wouldn't be any damn use to him if he passed out. He couldn't let himself lose it! If he was dead and Lauren tried to follow him, there would be no one to warn her. Behind him, as if down some tunnel, he faintly heard boots tapping on the rungs of a ladder. He plunged into the dark interior of the building.

FIFTEEN MINUTES after Bill left for Healdsburg, an officer from the Santa Rosa Police Department arrived at Lauren's office to take her statement and dust for prints. The uniformed officer looked confused when she told him the break-in was related to a sheriff's department case she'd been working on; he insisted she explain the whole thing while he took careful notes for his report. Lauren rather impatiently repeated the story, wishing Ramsey would call.

By the time the officer finished questioning her and opened up his evidence kit, Lauren realized Bill had been gone for over an hour. He'd left in a hurry, but she was sure he'd said he would call. Most likely he'd gotten caught up in talking with the plant manager and didn't want to interrupt the interview.

She called Ramsey's office again, but he was still tied up. Then she looked up the number of River Bend Lumber. A recording came on to tell her the number was no longer in service. She tried the other three lines listed for the plant, with the same response. As she hung up the phone, a wave of the most terrible apprehension swept through her.

"Julie," she said, "I'm going up to the River Bend Mill, where Bill is supposed to be doing that interview. When Captain Ramsey calls, tell him we've gone up there and all the phone lines are out. I don't like the feel of this at all."

OLD REDWOOD HIGHWAY was deserted as Lauren sped toward the mill. A beat-up truck passed her going the other way; it was the first vehicle she'd seen since turning off the highway five minutes before.

The first thing she saw of the River Bend Lumber Mill was the cyclone fence at the corner of the property. It rose eight feet from chalky ground along the drainage ditch, surmounted by corkscrews of barbed wire.

She pulled up short of the entrance and parked on the shoulder, wishing she'd had the foresight to keep her gun with her, instead of leaving it in the office where Sabrina could steal it. Like most P.I.'s she never carried a gun, but for the first time she felt naked without it as she stepped from the car and scanned the plant. She knew Ramsey would tell her she was a fool if she went in there alone and unarmed. But Bill was somewhere in the mill, and both her instinct and reason screamed that he was in trouble. She couldn't wait for more help to arrive before going in after him.

She ran lightly and silently onto the grounds, thankful she'd dressed in slacks and comfortable rubber-soled shoes. Except for Bill's car and one other parked beside it, the place was deserted. It was eerie. Conveyer belts and monorail tracks sprouted from the sides of buildings big enough to house sport stadiums. She felt distinctly as though she was stepping onto the set of some postnuclear science-fiction movie—all the people were gone, and only their forbidding, monolithic structures remained.

There was no sign of Bill or anyone else. Stepping onto the shack's porch, she noticed something had eaten into the wood at the corner. On the ground was a torn piece of siding with a dark stain on it. She looked more closely. The stain had to be blood! There were several holes in the tarmac where slugs had entered. From the angle, they appeared to have been fired from above. The whole scenario was becoming frighteningly clear: Bill had been ambushed!

There were more signs of blood on the ground. Lauren's stomach churned in fear. Had Bill known he was stepping into a trap? Surely he had, but he'd gone ahead, probably because he knew she was in danger and wanted to protect her. With her heart in her mouth she followed the trail of blood to a locked door in a nearby building. Bill had gone into this building and someone had bolted the door behind him. It was impossible to tell where he'd been hit or how badly, but there was a lot of blood on the ground. God, he could be inside there somewhere, bleeding to death. She had to find him fast. There must be another way to get in.

She ran, turned a corner, found another locked door, then ran what seemed like the length of a football field to the other end of the building and the millpond.

This end of the building sat directly on a small lake. A few mealy logs floated up against the wall. The water was stagnant and green, but it separated her from Bill, so she had to cross it. Using her arms for balance and keeping her eye out for soft spots, she made her way across the logs. She wobbled and almost fell in, then silently thanked her karate teacher for nagging her about perfecting her balance.

Two concave chutes that looked like log conveyers jutted from the mill into the pond. She jumped from the log onto the first trough and was halfway up it when she heard a creaking sound above her. Her gaze shot up. There was a second-story balcony straight ahead, and Sabrina Andersen emerged on it. She held a rifle loosely in her hands and her eyes scanned the pond. Lauren didn't wait for her to look down.

To the right of the trough she'd been climbing was a series of smaller, metal log conveyers that disappeared through big leather flaps into an addition to the mill. The covered opening was about fifteen feet wide, and she made for it. Struggling to keep her footing on the greased conveyers, Lauren scrambled up and pushed her way through the weather-beaten flaps.

It was completely dark inside, the only illumination coming from cracks between the flaps. But she didn't dare wait for her eyes to adjust to the dimness. Watching her feet by the light that filtered beneath the leather panels, she moved to the far wall.

She flattened herself against it, her heart beating faster as she tried to figure out where she was. Hope leapt in her that Bill might have taken refuge in the same spot, but as her eyes began to adjust, she could see only the log conveyers and another empty trough the size of a giant redwood. She seemed to have stumbled into the heart of one of the mill's processing operations, a place not intended for human beings, and she could see no exit except the way she'd come.

Lauren grimaced. The air was filled with a noxious, rotten-egg odor that was somehow familiar. But that didn't matter. She knew it would take Sabrina only a matter of seconds to come down the stairs from the balcony, climb down the trough and follow her in here. If she got lucky, Sabrina might nose the rifle through the leather flaps before entering, and she could grab the muzzle—

A loud electric hum filled the air and the wall behind her began to vibrate. *What the hell?* Sabrina must have gotten access to the building's power and turned it on.

She looked up. Through a glass panel above and across from her, she could vaguely make out a woman's head, probably in the machine's control room. Was that rotten-egg smell petroleum?

The hum intensified around her, and something stirred in Lauren's brain. Looking up at the metal and tubing apparatus that hung like a huge bat from the ceiling, she began backing up toward the flaps. As her hand reached behind her and groped at the opening, there was a gurgling sound, then water gushed from the overhead rig. Even as Lauren screamed and grabbed the leather flap for support, the memory that had been eluding her came clear. It was a documentary she'd once seen on the lumber industry, and she knew where she was: in the mill's debarker.

A combination of water and petroleum shot from overhead with all the power of a foursome of fire hoses, hitting the empty trough where Lauren knew a shaggy redwood log was supposed to lie. Her free hand rose to cover her eyes as the torrent ricocheted off the bare metal toward her, drenching her and nearly pounding her to her knees.

Blinded, she backed through the flaps, her feet slipping on the metal as she tried desperately to keep her footing. She half fell, half lowered herself to the narrow metal conveyer and slid down it to the outside trough.

Her wool jacket and slacks were sodden, but she was in one piece. Grabbing at her jacket, she found a part of the inside lining that wasn't wet and bent over to dry her eyes. When she looked up, her vision was blurry and she batted her eyes to try to clear them. She was surprised and thankful that they weren't burning.

She got up, calculated the distance to the other trough and jumped. She almost overleapt it and had to put her hands down to steady herself as she landed on the curved chute. She knew Sabrina would be out the door to the debarker at any moment. She ran up the trough, under a giant chain saw, and through the open hatchway into the mill.

At least now she was inside the building where Bill had gone. She stepped off the log conveyer and moved along the wall into the heavy darkness. There was no sign of Bill—no movement, no noise. From what she could see she was surrounded by heavy machinery and a maze of conveyers. Above her was the low ceiling of what appeared to be a second-story room; it ended maybe ten yards from where she stood and where the building opened up. There were no windows under the

second floor, but it seemed lighter beyond the overhang, where perhaps there were windows higher up.
The air smelled faintly like ginger.

She heard steps above, on the balcony outside, and
held her breath. Moments later, the footsteps approached the hatchway she'd just come through.
Moving farther into the darkness, Lauren tensed. But
Sabrina didn't appear. Instead, the doors swung closed
with a bang, and she could hear a padlock being inserted.

*What's Sabrina doing? Is she going to try to torch
the building, with me inside? And where's Bill?* Lauren shivered. When Sabrina appeared on the balcony,
she'd been relaxed, the rifle not poised as though she
expected to be fired on. Had she already shot Bill and
left him for dead somewhere in this dark, forbidding
barn?

Footsteps came overhead again, entering the story
above her. It was still possible Bill was alive, she told
herself. There was a chance he'd escaped and made his
way across the millpond before she'd gotten here. He
could be on his way to call the police right now. Pray
God it was true! She couldn't give up yet, especially
while there was a chance he was still alive.

Moving as quietly as she could, Lauren followed the
steps as they sounded above her. She had to detour
around one of the enormous saws, but she had no
difficulty keeping up with the slow footfalls.

As they approached the end of the second floor,
Lauren could see that a narrow wooden catwalk
stretched from it down the length of the mill to the far

wall. If Sabrina went out on the catwalk and Lauren remained directly underneath, Sabrina wouldn't be able to tell she was there.

This Lauren did. As she emerged from under the second floor, she saw it was indeed lighter here, easier to see. There were still no glass windows, but panels of yellowed fiberglass ran around the eaves, letting in a murky light. Unlighted fluorescent fixtures were suspended from the ceiling; great hanks of sawdust-covered cobwebs hung from them.

She remained directly below the catwalk as Sabrina continued her cautious advance. Lauren kept her eyes trained overhead, but when they flicked down, she could see she was approaching a mesh of conveyers that would be almost impossible to crawl over. *Come on baby, it's now or never,* she said in her head, urging Sabrina to do what she wanted. She reached down to her feet and picked up a wood chip, flicking it into the darkness. As it landed with a faint click, the nose of Sabrina's rifle appeared over the catwalk banister.

With a quick hand-up from one of the posts that supported the walkway, Lauren grabbed at the rifle and yanked with all her might. A muted cry was heard from above as the rifle came free into Lauren's hands.

She held the rifle between her knees as she quickly removed her jacket, then swung it out beyond the walkway where Sabrina would see it. There was no shot. As Lauren tossed the ruined garment aside, she felt confident that her opponent's only weapon now lay in her hands.

There was a stairway just behind her leading to the catwalk. As she emerged from her cover, Lauren kept her eyes trained on Sabrina. The woman stood surprisingly at ease, arms at her sides, and her expression was calm as Lauren ascended the stairs, rifle in the ready position at her hip.

Lauren paused about ten feet from the other woman and studied her for a moment. She wore a black jersey jumpsuit topped with a kind of tunic that fell straight from her breasts to just below her waist. Her feet were shod in black athletic shoes. The outfit gave her a look of feline efficiency and menace. It made Lauren feel slightly unnerved, and she focused on the woman's face. It was then that she realized the person before her was not, could not be, Sabrina Andersen. The nose, the eyes, the mouth, were all different. For coloring and size this woman and Sabrina could have been twins, but close up there was no facial resemblance whatsoever.

Lauren gasped as the full realization of who stood before her hit her. Fear spiked up her back and she said, "Where's Bill Donelan?"

"You're in less of a position to dictate than you know," the woman said. Sardonic amusement fired sparks in her black eyes. "But just so you'll die happy, I'll tell you the truth. Your brave Mr. Donelan ran away. But don't worry—" her lip curled "—I'll get him next time."

Anger made Lauren flash the muzzle of the rifle down to a point between them and pull the trigger.

Nothing happened.

Lauren had only a stupefied split second to wonder what had gone wrong before the woman in black lunged for her. Her hands stretched before her, fingers curled like the claws of a cat, and she crabbed toward Lauren in what was forbiddingly similar to a karate stance. Lauren threw the useless firearm aside just in time to grab her attacker's wrists in a two-handed hold. As they struggled, the rifle clattered over the edge of the catwalk and fell into the bowels of the machinery.

Lauren's opponent pulled back on her left foot and swung her hands violently outward. Lauren tried to force the woman's arms back between them. As she pushed, the woman suddenly gave in and collapsed her hands back together, then grasped Lauren's left wrist in her left hand, crossing Lauren's arms at the wrists. Before Lauren could react, she felt a sharp pain as the other's left knee came up, punching her in the crotch.

Lauren let go with a gasp and backed off, pain spiking through her groin. The hellcat was right on top of her, seizing her blouse at the shoulder and jerking downward, forcing her to bend at the waist. Then the woman's fist came down, jackhammer hard, on her back, punctuated by a bloodcurdling karate yell.

Lauren coughed and staggered, her heart fibrillating from the force of the blow. She almost went down on her bad knee but caught the banister and steadied herself. Instinct screamed at her to run—but she was still held fast by her blouse. She had to get away!

Lauren swung her hand in a knife-edged blow, hitting the woman's tender forearm and forcing her to let go. She followed it with an uppercut directed at the woman's chin, but failed to make contact. Nevertheless, she was able to scramble backward before the demon could grab her again.

Lauren would have turned tail and run, but her attacker didn't come after her, and curiosity made Lauren pause at a wary distance and study her opponent. Lauren's breath came in ragged gasps, but the woman in black wasn't even puffing. She crouched in an easy, natural bow stance, as if waiting for Lauren to make the next move.

Whoever this woman was she'd studied with a real martial arts master, Lauren was sure. This wasn't the kind of traditional karate Lauren knew, but a full-contact, aggressive, street-fighting version. Fear snaked through Lauren's stomach, leaving her insides cold.

Her attacker's eyes were bright and her right cheek gave a tic, like the reflexive twitch of a cat's whiskers. Instinctively Lauren's muscles tensed and she took a step backward, then bolted down the stairs into the shadows.

From her hiding place in the darkness behind one of the saws, Lauren watched as the woman in black disappeared down the catwalk into the second-story room at the end of it. A small sign next to the doorway read Saw Shop.

Lauren tried to clear her head, to figure out what to do next before the woman reappeared, perhaps with a fresh weapon, and came looking for her.

The minute she'd seen the woman's face and realized she wasn't Sabrina but an impersonator, Lauren felt sure she must be a paid killer. If she'd had time to think it through, Lauren was sure all the facts would fall into place. The woman's lethal karate skills surely confirmed her as a professional assassin, hired to impersonate Sabrina and to frame her for the murder of Nat, and now Lauren and Bill. It was obvious the woman had allowed Lauren to take the unloaded gun from her because she wanted to kill her in hand-to-hand combat and make it look as though Sabrina had done it.

Lauren shuddered. The thought that Bill had gotten out alive was her only comfort. Thank God! Even if she didn't make it, he had. It was miles by foot to the nearest phone, but there was still a slim chance he might summon help in time to save her, too.

A small sound, like the whine of a cat, made the hair stand up on Lauren's neck. She swiveled around, hands before her ready to strike. When the sound came again, more human than animal, and strangely familiar, a doubly fearful suspicion rose in her heart.

Keeping low so the assassin wouldn't see her, Lauren moved around the saw, back to where one of the long conveyers flanked a wall. On the floor, wedged between the machinery and the wall, was the body of Bill Donelan.

HE WAS UNCONSCIOUS, his breathing quiet but shallow except for the delirious moan she'd heard. Lauren reached out to touch his head, then took back her hand, fearful of hurting him. Dear God, there was a lot of blood; it was matted in his hair and soaked into the collar of his shirt. Forcing herself not to panic, she picked up his limp wrist and felt his pulse. The skin was clammy, the heartbeat slow. Lauren slumped down next to him, holding his hand in both of hers. She could just picture him crawling in here in the darkness, seeking a safe hiding place as he felt himself slip from consciousness. She wanted to cry, but she couldn't, or she'd give away their hiding place.

She pinched the skin between her eyes. Why couldn't Bill have gotten out?

Then the mill whined to life.

All around them, giant machines suddenly growled and ground into action. Conveyers lurched forward, circular saw blades the size of record albums spun, and ten-foot-high band saws gyrated.

Lauren clamped her hands to her ears. She suddenly knew exactly what her pursuer was doing. *She was driving her.*

The woman in black had planned everything, carefully engineered it from the beginning. She'd given Lauren time to search for another exit, then thrown the master switch to the building's power.

Her attacker was driving her, like an animal from the bush. There was only one way out of this building, and the killer intended for her to take it—through the saw shop, *where she was waiting.*

Frantically Lauren searched Bill's holster and his coat pockets. Where was his gun? She felt around his body but couldn't find it.

Lauren sat back on her heels and hid her face in her hands as she suppressed a sob. In her soul she knew she couldn't fight that woman and win, not even if she'd been a third-degree black belt. But Bill was hurt, badly. In the dark it was impossible to tell what had caused the head wound. That broken piece of siding could have fractured his skull, or there could be a bullet lodged in his brain. He might have other, internal injuries she couldn't see. She couldn't wait here and let him bleed to death. She had to try to bring their attacker down and get them both out of here.

Squinting through the dust-filled air, she saw the woman in black at the door to the saw shop, looking out over the factory, searching for her.

She and Bill had only one chance, and she had to take it. Lauren flexed her aching shoulder muscles, then stood stiffly. With faltering steps, she headed for the stairs.

As Lauren gained the catwalk, the woman gracefully backed up until she stood in the middle of the second-story room, arms folded across her chest. Lauren paused in the doorway to get her bearings.

There was a wooden floor in the large, bare shop, punctuated with bolts that protruded from the floor where machinery had once stood. Empty, scarred workbenches and cabinets lined the walls. The air was filled with dust, but it was much brighter here than below; high up, beneath the eaves, were glass-paned windows. A door to the outside balcony and freedom stood tantalizingly ajar in the far wall.

She forced her eyes to focus on the calm, almost smug face of her attacker, and her skin crawled. The thought that this mysterious woman had killed Nat, had nearly killed Suzie and was bent on murdering her repelled Lauren, but she knew she had to keep her eyes on her face every moment. A fraction of a second before striking, the woman's facial muscles would tighten, and Lauren knew she desperately needed that small advantage to stay alive.

She resisted an automatic, ludicrous urge to bow to her opponent and went into her neutral bow stance. With slow, almost leisurely movements, her opponent unfolded her limbs in a similar posture and stepped forward. It was as though the damn woman was in no hurry—she had all day to kill her!

Lauren's fear subsided as anger welled up in its place, and without preamble she advanced.

The killer was swift, as well as powerful. Lauren took a left reverse punch straight into her breast. Pain flared out over her chest and shoulders, then her torso went numb. Ignoring the pain and violation she felt, she refused to take her eyes from her opponent's.

Lauren abandoned her offensive posture and fell into a defensive strategy. Her karate teacher had always praised her for her devotion to the *katas*, the traditional movements practiced in response to an invisible partner's attacks—a kind of shadowboxing. Lauren's body knew dozens of *katas*, and now that she needed them, she hoped they wouldn't desert her.

Knowing that the best place to be when a blow lands is somewhere else, Lauren concentrated on evading the other woman, blocking her leg kicks and punches when she couldn't move away fast enough.

After a long two minutes of fighting, Lauren was still holding her own. Only one out of three of the woman's blows were connecting, boosting Lauren's confidence and allowing her to calm her mind. As her fear subsided, her subconscious began to take the ascendancy, enabling her to respond more quickly than her conscious mind could have. Sweat poured off her, but she didn't notice as her hand swept the beads from her forehead. She lost track of time. There was no room in her thoughts for what had been or what might be. There was only the now and the instinctive instructions to parry, block, evade.

She was doing an ever better job of dodging the other's blows. Her opponent's face began to scrunch up in a look of surprise and frustration, like a cat with an unexpectedly exuberant mouse. Lauren hoped her attacker's frustration would interfere with her concentration. And when she saw her chance, Lauren took it.

She came in with a roundhouse punch that connected with a satisfying crack of the woman's jaw. Her opponent's garbled grunt of fury preceded a left high kick aimed at Lauren's head. Instead of retreating this time, Lauren unexpectedly stepped in with a high block, throwing the killer off balance, then delivered a neat knee-strike to the stomach. The woman in black stumbled; as she did, Lauren pivoted at the waist, propelling her enemy forward. To make sure she went all the way down, she added an elbow strike to the back.

With triumph, Lauren watched her attacker crash to the floor, apparently sickened and dizzy. If she wanted to kill the murderous woman, Lauren realized, now was her chance to do it. She could give her one quick, deadly blow, and everyone would think it was self-defense. No dragging court trial, no endless appeals; and Nat and Suzie would be avenged.

At the thought of her wounded sister, the karate cry flew to Lauren's throat and her right hand went up in a knife edge, poised to strike at the woman's outstretched neck.

Then her hand fell to her side and she stepped back.

It took Lauren a moment to think straight again. The anger had been so intense it left her feeling shaken, her hands trembling. The woman in black lay at her feet, moaning slightly, probably from the blow she'd taken in the stomach.

Lauren backed off and allowed the wounded woman to catch her breath. She was in obvious pain, and her left arm hung limply at a crooked angle. As Lauren bent to grab her arm, the woman raised her good hand and begged, "No, please. My shoulder, hell, I think it's broken.... I'm going to be sick." She half rose and staggered over to one of the tall, built-in closets. She leaned heavily against it, her breath coming in labored gulps.

Lauren decided to tie the woman up and and leave her for the police. There was no time to waste. She needed to get to her car and find a phone where she could call an ambulance for Bill. She glanced around for something to bind her prisoner with. When she looked back a moment later, the cabinet door was open, and the woman in black had a chain saw in her hands.

The saw throbbed to life as Lauren cursed her gullibility and retreated backward. The woman laughed and pursued her, the saw held before her in hands that were menacingly strong and steady.

Lauren had no time to look behind her, and she tripped over one of the bolts in the floor. The stumble saved her life as the saw passed harmlessly within a millimeter of her midriff. The woman wielded the saw in two hands like a medieval broadsword, this time aiming at Lauren's head.

Because the machine was heavy and awkward, it came around more slowly than a karate blow would have, giving Lauren the time she needed to regain her balance and duck.

She knew she had to avoid the saw without allowing the woman to force her back into one of the shop's corners.

As the killer tried a slicing technique, Lauren scurried to the side. The woman bared her teeth, growling with rage at the missed blow, and her fury seemed to fuel her strength so that she swung with greater speed and fierceness. Lauren managed barely to sidestep her once more, but she knew it was only a matter of time until the ragged, blurred teeth of the saw met her flesh.

Her only hope was to kick the saw from the woman's hands. It was a very slim chance, but if she used her longest weapon, her leg, in a front kick, she might be able to do it. If she miscalculated, the saw would take her leg off, or she could lose her balance and fall to the floor.

Lauren backed up, preparing to kick, and stepped on one of the errant floor bolts. She twisted violently, tried to regain her balance, but went down, landing hard on her weakened right knee.

Pain exploded in her kneecap and she cried out. She tried to rise, but the woman was coming after her with the saw, a laugh of triumph bubbling from her thin lips. Lauren pushed herself along the floor with her good leg, trying desperately to escape.

Chapter Fourteen

Lauren was dead, and she knew it. She rolled frantically to the side but couldn't get away. The woman raised the saw and Lauren braced herself for the blow.

"Stop!"

Lauren's heart almost obeyed the shouted command. Through her attacker's legs, she saw Bill running down the catwalk toward them.

The dark-haired woman cursed and hesitated. Lauren scuttled backward another foot. The saw came whining down, eating into the boards where Lauren's legs had been.

Bill slid to a stop in the doorway, feet apart, automatic held forward in both hands. The gun barked and the killer staggered, a bullet in her right shoulder. With a cry of outrage, she hoisted the saw with her left arm and rushed at Bill.

Bill's eyes widened in disbelief. She was almost on top of him when he fired again. The shot hurled her body backward, off her feet and down onto the shop floor. The saw flew to the left, thudding on the floor and throwing up splinters until the engine coughed and then went silent.

Bill remained hunched, pistol trained on the prone figure, as he called to Lauren, "Are you hurt?"

"No. I just fell on my knee. I'm fine."

"Thank God."

The woman in black didn't move, and her eyes stared at the ceiling, but her ragged breathing was clearly audible. Bill cautiously frisked her for hidden weapons before going to Lauren and helping her up. He folded her in his arms and pressed her head against his neck. "Thank God," he repeated.

Tears of joy that Bill was alive and all right flowed from Lauren's eyes.

"If I'd stayed unconscious down there another second she would have had you," Bill said. "I would never have forgiven myself." He kissed her hair. "I love you, Lauren."

"I love you, too." She burrowed closer into his shoulder. She'd been so near to dying, and now she was safe, wonderfully safe in Bill's arms. Intense relief swept through her, made her want to laugh, but she didn't seem to have the breath for it yet.

Bill must have felt the same way, because after a minute of tenderly stroking her back he began to chuckle. "I knew you were a good investigator, sweetheart, but this was the one time I hoped you'd be fooled. I didn't want you following me up to the mill, but somehow I suspected you would."

"And whose idea was it to risk your neck in the first place?" Lauren looked up at him in mock reproof.

"The next time you want to show how much you care, flowers will be enough!"

Bill threw back his head and laughed. "At least you're not accusing me of leaving you behind! I wouldn't want you to think I'm a chauvinist or something."

"No, just thickheaded. I hope. How *is* your head?" She tilted his chin to inspect the wound. "It looks awful."

"I've got one hell of a headache, but it's just a superficial wound."

"You're going to need stitches," Lauren said dubiously, "and you may well have a concussion."

Bill shrugged one shoulder as he released her. "Come on. I think our friend here is hit bad. We'd better try to talk to her."

Lauren pursed her lips, but followed suit as Bill crouched down beside the fallen killer. The woman's eyes had closed. Blood oozed from the left side of her chest and a foamy trickle of blood came from her mouth.

Bill grimaced, rubbing imaginary dirt from his palms. Lauren thought he must be regretting having had to shoot her, but what else could he have done? It was either Bill or the assassin, and Lauren knew which *she* preferred.

Bill took off his coat and wadded up one of the sleeves. Lauren took it from him and held it hard against the wound. Feeling the pressure, the woman opened her eyes, and Lauren read fear in them. Despite herself, Lauren said almost kindly, "We'll try to stop the bleeding. Don't move."

Surprise flickered in the dark eyes.

"We know you're a professional," Bill said quietly but firmly. "Tell us who hired you."

The woman's brow puckered, but she didn't speak.

"Talk to us," Bill urged. "You've got nothing to lose now. Was it Caine?"

At first, Lauren didn't think the woman would speak, then she murmured, "Y-yes. It was Chuck Caine."

Lauren and Bill exchanged a look.

"Do you know why?" Bill said.

"Industrial..." She closed her eyes for a moment as a spasm went through her chest. Lauren tried to steady her, holding the compress tight, as she coughed. With effort, she caught her breath and finished. "Industrial espionage. Andersen stole the voice... processor plans from Caine."

Another spasm convulsed her body. The woman's eyes opened wide, then closed. And suddenly, she was gone.

"Damn!" Bill said.

"WE'RE GOING to have trouble nailing Caine with only that woman's dying confession as evidence," Bill said as they walked out to his parked car.

Lauren squeezed his arm. "We can talk about it while we drive you to the nearest hospital."

"First I've got a feeling about that car," Bill said. He steered her toward the assassin's rental car and rapped on the trunk. A muffled response came from inside.

Lauren's brows flew up. "Sabrina?"

"Uh-huh, and alive I'm glad to say. I wasn't sure if she would be. I've got a crowbar in the back."

A few minutes later Bill had popped the trunk and a groggy Sabrina was being loosened from her bonds and gag.

"Lord, my head aches," Sabrina said as she stood unsteadily by the car. Her purple-and-black velour pullover and matching pants were crumpled, but otherwise she seemed to be no worse for wear. "Where am I? What happened?"

"Don't be alarmed, Mrs. Andersen," Bill said. "Lauren and I look pretty beat-up, but you're among friends, and the woman who abducted you won't be coming back. Do you remember what happened to you?"

"Just that I was shopping in the mall when I felt a sharp pain, as though someone stabbed me with a needle from behind. When I woke up, I was all tied up in there." She massaged her wrists.

Now that Sabrina had gotten some fresh air and cleared her head, Lauren thought her eyes looked brighter, more focused than she'd ever seen them.

"I know you two, don't I?" Sabrina said. "Aren't you the woman who was with my husband at the Vineyard?"

"Yes, Mrs. Andersen. I'm a private investigator, and this is my associate, Bill Donelan."

Sabrina turned her gaze to Bill. "The insurance man?"

He smiled. "That's me. We've been on the trail of the woman who killed your husband and kidnapped you. We'll be happy to explain everything later, Mrs. Andersen, but if we're going to catch your husband's killer, time is of the essence, and I need to ask you some questions. Were you aware Nat was involved in industrial espionage?"

"No." Tears welled up in Sabrina's eyes. "I'm not really surprised, though. Nat was so obsessive about his work, so competitive. But I had no idea."

"Did he ever mention the name Chuck Caine to you?" Lauren asked.

"I know he's another computer manufacturer, but that's all. You see, Nat and I never talked much. We were only married a few months when I realized he didn't love me. He'd only married me to put up the sort of facade his business associates expected. At first I thought it was another woman, but then one day, I found something in Nat's bedroom. He didn't know I'd gone in. It was a foreign magazine, with pictures of..." Her voice broke. "They were so young...it turned my stomach. Our chauffeur used to drive Nat into San Francisco every Friday night. I didn't know where he went. Dirk was too ashamed to tell me, and he hated Nat because of it."

Lauren put her arm around Sabrina as the woman began to cry. Over Sabrina's head she regarded Bill with a grim expression. "No wonder Dirk wouldn't talk to us. I remember how edgy he was down in Pebble Beach—he must have sensed Nat was afraid someone was after him. When Nat was killed, Dirk probably figured he'd gotten his just deserts."

"And it confirms my suspicion he hired you because he needed a bodyguard. With Caine's reputation for settling scores personally, Nat probably expected him to walk up to him with a gun." He turned to Sabrina. "Mrs. Andersen, let's get you into the car and we'll drive you home."

Lauren helped him settle Sabrina in the back of the Taurus. They looked up at the sound of sirens. A moment later three squad cars turned into the main gate with a screech of tires.

Lauren smiled wryly. "I thought the cavalry always arrived just in time in those old movies of yours."

The first car slid to a stop behind Bill's Taurus, and Captain Ramsey jumped out. "I left as soon as your secretary got hold of me," he said breathlessly. His eyes started as he took in Lauren's soggy, grimy outfit and Bill's bloodied head. "What in the hell has been going on here?"

Bill slid his arm around Lauren and grinned. "I know we look like something out of *Night of the Living Dead,* but we're really okay."

"The hell you are," Ramsey said, and called back over his shoulder, "Have that paramedic unit move up!"

"I HOPE THIS PLAN of ours works," Lauren said later that evening as Bill drove them along a back country road over the foothills between Santa Rosa and Rohnert Park. A neat bandage covered Bill's left temple, and they both wore fresh clothing. Above them, a quarter moon was obscured by clouds as they turned onto the narrow two-lane road leading to Chuck Caine's home. The only illumination, besides their headlights, came from a van that made the turn behind them.

"Are you scared?" Bill asked. "Be honest. You don't have to go with me if you are."

"No way! I wouldn't miss this for the world."

Bill smiled proudly in the dark and patted her leg.

"I'm glad we're finally winding this up," she admitted. "It's not only been the most dangerous case I've ever worked, it's been the most puzzling. Nothing has turned out to be as it first seemed—Nat's character, the nature of Sabrina's mental problems, the motive for Nat's murder. Not to mention the misunderstandings between the two of us."

Bill smiled and squeezed her hand. "Well, we may have been misled along the way, but finding out the truth in the end is what matters."

"I can't help feeling stupid that Nat took me in so completely."

"He was a good actor," Bill said. "He had a lot of people fooled."

"I guess you're right. From what Sabrina said, it's clear now why he was content with a sham marriage." Lauren shuddered. "No wonder he was so upset when Sabrina found him with me in the restaurant—a scandalous divorce from a rich and compliant wife who didn't complain about his neglect was probably the last thing Nat wanted.''

Bill grunted, then leaned forward, staring through the glass. "Here it is.'' He took a sharp right onto the private road, and the bumpy asphalt immediately smoothed out beneath their wheels. The headlights picked out the stark forms of a dozen olive trees that lined the drive, and within moments they got their first glimpse of a large ranch-style house of brick and natural redwood, bathed in soft floodlights. As they pulled up, Lauren could see lights shining in the draped windows to the right of the front door.

"I hope that means he's home,'' she said. She glanced at the clock in the dash. It was almost nine.

"Planning his next move, no doubt,'' Bill said. "Let's go.''

When they stepped out of the car, Bill pulled his sport jacket from the back seat and straightened his tie. Lauren was wearing jeans, but she told herself grimly that if her appearance didn't impress Caine, what she had to tell him undoubtedly would.

Bill took her reassuringly by the arm and they walked to the front door, where Bill pressed the bell. Lauren glanced back down the drive behind them, but the grounds were dark and still.

In less than a minute the porch light flicked on and the door opened, revealing the backlit, bulldoglike figure of Chuck Caine.

As Lauren willed her eyes to adjust to the light, she could see he was casually dressed in slacks and a burgundy fisherman's sweater. He regarded them with an innocent, questioning look that made Lauren sick with anger.

"Mr. Hart, isn't it?" Caine said. He gave a bemused smile. "It's a little late for a magazine interview, don't you think?"

"I'm a private investigator, Mr. Caine," Bill said dryly. "I think you know Ms. Pierce."

When Caine frowned with perplexity, Lauren said tightly, "We've never been introduced, but we know each other."

Caine's expression remained uncertain, but he stepped back and stretched one arm toward the living room. "Why don't you come in."

They followed him into the adjoining room, which was carefully decorated in early American from the muslin curtains at the windows to the wing chairs and braided rugs on the polished hardwood floor.

"Do you have a family, Mr. Caine?" Lauren asked, hoping no one was asleep upstairs.

"Yes," he replied over his shoulder as he headed for a bar at the back of the room. "Two grown children and three grandchildren. My wife's out of town. Can I offer you something to drink?"

"I don't think we'll have time, Mr. Caine, but thank you," Bill answered.

Lauren thought Caine seemed completely relaxed. Was he putting on a show to unnerve them? Bill didn't seem to be sweating—maybe he'd figured out the other man already.

"Please, sit down," Caine urged, as he poured himself a scotch.

Bill sat down on the flame-stitched camelback sofa, still facing their host, and Lauren followed his lead. Caine crossed to sit on the matching love seat opposite them and took a sip of his drink.

Lauren mentally braced herself as Bill began to speak.

"Before I tell you why we're here, Mr. Caine, I just want to say I admire you, in a grim sort of way. When you found out Nat Andersen had stolen your plans for the voice processor and was rushing it onto the market ahead of you, you decided to take your revenge on him and perhaps buy his company from his heirs in the process. Were you telling the truth when you said Andersen's brothers aren't willing to sell Micom?"

Caine smiled secretively. "I've no idea what you mean about stolen plans and revenge, but it's true that I've had some success convincing the Andersen brothers to reconsider selling."

Bill nodded. "But the part I admire most is how you fooled Nat Andersen by putting aside your lifelong principle of settling scores personally and sending a hired killer after him.

"Hiring a woman was brilliant. You must have had it planned even then to frame Sabrina Andersen if the police didn't accept the murder as an accident. But I think you were hoping to convince them it *was* an accident—your woman cased out the Andersen home so carefully, sneaking into the garage on the night when she knew the chauffeur would be off and rigging the car so there'd be no spilling of brake fluid on the garage floor to tip off the authorities. You wanted it to look like Andersen missed a turn on the road or fell asleep at the wheel. You must have gotten a fright when you learned Andersen took the butler with him on his last ride. I'm surprised you didn't get to Hinshaw in the hospital to stop him from coming out of the coma and telling the world Andersen's brakes had failed." Bill paused and eyed Caine. "How am I doing so far?"

Caine grimaced over his drink. "You've got a fantastic imagination, Donelan, not to mention a libelous one. But go on, you've piqued my curiosity."

"As soon as the butler regained consciousness, you put your plan to frame Sabrina into full motion. Your assassin had already been busy studying Lauren's movements, observing her feeding the neighbor's cat each evening in the unlocked garage, and she hid there and jumped Lauren, intentionally fumbling the attempt to make it look amateurish and leaving behind the scent of an expensive perfume. As you'd hoped, Lauren became convinced it was a jealous Sabrina who'd attacked her."

Bill glanced at Lauren, and with the eagerness of a performer stepping on stage, she took up the narrative. "You waited for me to go to the authorities and have Sabrina arrested, but when it didn't happen, you got the idea to send your paid killer to wait for me outside the parking garage and ram my car, instructing her to make sure that the bystanders got a good look at her long, black hair and slender figure as she fled so they could describe her to the police.

"When Sabrina wasn't immediately arrested and when you learned it wasn't me but my sister you'd almost killed, you must have gotten really desperate. You kidnapped Sabrina in the shopping mall, stole my files and computer disks on the case and trashed my office so it would look like a raving, insane Sabrina had done it. Then you tried to lure me to the mill where your assassin was to make it look like Sabrina and I had died in some violent struggle."

Caine scowled, and his words came out in a growl. "The two of you should write cheap fiction. You've got the minds for it."

"It's more than imagination, Caine," Lauren said. "We're here to make a citizen's arrest. Your hired killer was taken into custody this afternoon. She talked, Caine. She named you as her employer. The sheriff's deputies are probably on their way here now, but I got wind of it first, and since it's my sister you nearly killed, I'm going to have the pleasure of bringing you in."

Caine gave her a little, condescending smile. "I'm sorry to disappoint you, Lauren, but I have no intention of going with you to the sheriff's office." With a quick movement he withdrew a small revolver from between the cushions of the sofa next to him and indicated with a jerky movement of the barrel that they should raise their hands, which they did.

"I appreciate your dropping in to let me know the police are coming," Caine said, his fat lips twisting in a smile. "Your remarks about my ingenuity are flattering, but I'm afraid I can't return them. You'd have been much smarter to let the police handle things at this point. Now you'll have to pay for your stupidity with your lives."

Caine jerked to his feet and extended the arm with the gun toward them, the barrel pointed directly at Lauren's head. "Ladies first," he intoned with mock sweetness.

There was a sudden brittle crescendo around them as the living room's mullioned windows exploded inward. At the same time, the front door burst from its hinges and a man swathed in black and camouflage green, bearing an automatic rifle, jumped into the hall.

Lauren dropped to the floor as Bill flung himself over her, using his body to shield her from the shower of glass. Caine's knees bent as though to run and his gaze darted around the room. The pistol remained outstretched before him, but the arm that held it shook.

"Drop the gun, Caine!" the man in the hall commanded, "We've got you covered from all sides!"

The muzzles of a dozen rifles poked through the broken windows, their bearers almost invisible in black, bulletproof vests. Caine's eyes flicked once more over the room, and his tongue passed over his dry lips.

"Every man here is a crack shot, Caine," their leader yelled as he brought his own rifle to his eye. "If you don't want to go to the morgue in a dozen pieces, you'd better drop the gun *now!*''

With a disgusted sigh, Caine's arm fell to his side, and the gun dropped to the sofa behind him. Immediately the team leader closed in on him, pulling a set of handcuffs from the pocket of his baggy fatigues.

Lauren let out her breath in a rush and almost laughed, she was so relieved. Bill helped her up from the floor and then wrapped her in his arms.

''Good job, kid,'' he whispered, releasing her.

''Good job,'' she repeated, returning his triumphant smile.

''You two okay?''

Bill kept one arm around Lauren as he turned to greet Captain Ramsey. ''Yes, we're fine.'' He eyed Caine, who was standing stiffly as the officer adjusted his handcuffs. ''I'm just a little uncomfortable.'' Bill removed his sport coat and unbuttoned his shirt to reveal a remote microphone strapped around his hairy midriff. ''This thing itches like hell. Good thing it works so well.'' He gave Caine a toothy grin before the officer jerked his prisoner around and began reading him his rights.

Ramsey nodded at Bill. ''I was listening out in the van and we picked up everything loud and clear. Him threatening you and pulling a gun on you was as good as a signed confession. There's no way in God's green earth Caine can escape prison now.''

''I've got to call my mother and Allen,'' Lauren said. ''I want to tell them we've caught the people who hurt Suzie. It's late, but I know they've been waiting to hear from me. Is there a phone around here?''

"Yes, but you'll have to wait." The corners of Bill's mouth twitched. "I think Caine's using it to call his lawyer."

Chapter Fifteen

Lauren put her arm around Suzie's shoulders as the photographer insisted on taking just one more picture of them together.

The garlanded reception hall was bursting with a happy crowd of Pierce relations and friends. As the photographer nodded and stepped away to snap the guests, Lauren lifted the veil back from her sister's ear and whispered, "You're the most beautiful bride ever, Suz."

Beneath the cap decorated with silk roses that the bride had designed herself, Suzie's face was radiant. Several plastic surgeries over a period of months had done miracles, and the surgeon had assured them that, with time, even the hairline scars would fade.

"If you ask me," Suzie said, "*you're* the most elegant bride here, sis. You were right when we first saw that gown in the shop window—it was made for you."

"Do you think so?" Lauren glanced down at the slim lace-covered skirt.

"Yes, it's perfection, just like everything else today." Suzie's eyes shone. "It's been so much fun planning this double wedding with you."

"I wouldn't have missed it for anything, either, but you'll have to thank my new business partner for giving me the time off," Lauren said.

"Actually," Suzie said, "I have to confess I had something to do with arranging that."

"You did?"

"Yes. You see, you two had so much work following the publicity from the Andersen case, not to mention all the D.A.'s stuff, that I suggested Bill bring up a couple of the guys he worked with in L.A. to help out."

"So that's where he got the idea! Well, I'm in your debt, honey."

"You know," Suzie said, growing serious, "I used to get nightmares about the crash, but I haven't had one for weeks now. And if it hadn't been for the accident, we would have missed doing this together."

Lauren felt tears start in her eyes. Suzie had never blamed her for the crash, and turning a tragedy into a blessing in disguise was so like her.

"Speaking of your new partner," Suzie said, "here he comes now."

Bill and Allen walked up, resplendent in black, double-breasted tuxedos, starched dress shirts and bow ties. Bill put his arms around his new wife and kissed her. "Have I told you I love you today?" he asked, his eyes wandering adoringly over her features.

"Yes, more times than I can count, but I like it, so don't stop. By the way—" she reached up on tiptoe to kiss his nose "—I love you, too."

A jeweled wedding crown was nestled in Lauren's upswept hair. Bill nuzzled her ear, threatening to dislodge the diamond earrings he'd given her the night before as a wedding present. "This dress is so beautiful," he breathed, "that I can't wait to take it off you."

Lauren patted his satin lapel with her gloved hand and made her lips pouty in remonstrance, but there was a spark in her aqua eyes that matched his own.

Bill sighed with resigned impatience, then turned to kiss his new sister-in-law on the cheek. With a mischievous smile he asked Suzie, "So, are you glad Sylvester Stallone didn't come to steal you away, after all?"

Suzie was nodding when Allen said, "Oh, but he did!"

Three pairs of amazed eyes turned on Allen.

"I sat outside the girls' condo all last night," Allen said. "When Sly pulled up, I told him he wasn't making love to my girl! We went a few rounds on the grass, then he got back in his Porsche with a bloody nose and drove off."

Suzie was transported with laughter as Bill clapped Allen on the back. A waiter offered his tray, and they each took a glass of champagne.

Lauren held hers aloft as she winked up at Bill. "Believe me, Suzie," she said, "there's nothing like having a man who'll risk his life for you."

Bill raised his glass to Lauren's as he pulled her close to his side. "Or having a woman worth fighting for."

"Here, here," Allen said, and they all drank the toast.